The collected works of Edward Austin Dodd, a Jamaican writer in the early 20th century

Edited by

Rosemary A. Dodd
and
Robert B. Barker

Introduction by Rosemary A. Dodd

In memory of

Beverley, Jocelyn,

and Philip

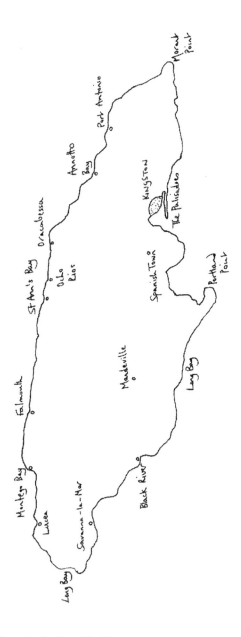

Fig. 1 Map of Jamaica by R.A. Dodd

CONTENTS

ACKNOWLEDGMENTS

This book would not exist without the support of Robert Barker. I am enormously grateful to him for the research he carried out on my behalf and for his help with my own research – his laser-like questions always kept me on my toes – and for all his unwavering support.

I am most grateful to Robert, Mike and Chrissie Webb who all read my introduction and made helpful suggestions. A huge thankyou is owed to Sally Barker for getting the illustrations into publishable form and to Anne Maclachlan for her insights into poetry. I am indebted to Dr. Richard Smith of Goldsmiths, University of London, who helped me better understand the Jamaica that Eddie Dodd lived in, and for his encouragement.

I am also grateful to Nicole Prawl at the National Library of Jamaica who provided the pages from the *Jamaica Times* that I could not find at the British Library, and to Daniel Hutchings for supplying the photo of Norah Shaw's painting for the cover.

All illustrations by Edward Austin Dodd
unless otherwise stated.

1 PERSONAL FOREWORD

One day in 2016, Robert Barker, a Jamaican friend and consummate historian, asked me if I knew who E. A. Dodd, a published writer in Jamaica, was. Thinking of my mother, Elizabeth Anne Dodd, who had written many letters to and some articles for *The Gleaner* in the 1970s, I replied, "Yes, of course." I had no idea that my great uncle Edward Austin Dodd (1882-1917) had written short stories or that they had been published. (I had known that he had painted, for at least one of his watercolours had survived and was amongst family papers.) Robert proceeded to enlighten me. In Frank Cundall's *Supplement to Bibliographia Jamaicensis* published in 1908 was the entry: '607 – *MAROON MEDICINE. By* E. Snod [E. A. Dodd]. All Jamaica Library No. 2. 1905.'

Robert found a digitised copy of *Maroon Medicine* in the University of Florida's online digital library. We read and enjoyed the four stories it contained. Robert discovered that *Maroon Medicine* had been written about by some scholars of early Jamaican literature. One online paper mentioned another short story, *Farder Matney's Pigs*; another said that E. A. Dodd had also written poems.

We were determined to find everything we could that my great uncle had written. Robert searched the online archive of *The Gleaner.* I pored over microfilm copies of the *Jamaica Times* at the British Library. We liked what we found – both the writing and the person we discovered through his fiction and non-fiction.

Edward "Eddie" Austin Dodd was my paternal grandfather's younger brother. Eddie died in 1917 and my father was not born until 1922 so they never knew one another. My father and his brother and sister had a passion for researching and discussing their family history. Ironically, despite tracing various ancestral lines for several centuries, surprisingly little was known by my family about their closest relatives. Certainly no one in the family remembered that Eddie had been a published writer.

Eddie's works appeared in both *The Gleaner* and in the *Jamaica Times*, the latter under the editorship of Thomas Henry MacDermot ("Tom Redcam"). His stories are very Jamaican and reflect his upbringing in rural Jamaica. It is clear that Eddie had acute powers of observation, an ear for the local Jamaican dialect, and an ability to transfer what he heard into print, along with an interest in and love of Jamaican people.

Robert and I discovered that Eddie had been a railway engineer, following in the footsteps of both his father and his elder brother. He was also a scholar, a sportsman, an artist, and an illustrator, as well as a writer of poems, commentaries, travelogues, and short stories.

Edward Austin Dodd's relatively short life spanned the last 18 years of the nineteenth century and the first 17 of the twentieth century. He did not leave a large published legacy but we believe that his work is worth republishing and his story worth telling.

The Collected Works of Edward Austin Dodd

2 JAMAICA IN 1882

Edward Austin Dodd was born in 1882, 44 years after the full emancipation of the enslaved people of Jamaica in 1838. This was also 17 years after the "Morant Bay Rebellion" of 1865, an event that brought about great changes in the colony. He came of age shortly after the turn of the century when the banana export economy had transformed the fortunes of the island.

At emancipation, plantation owners were compensated by the British Government for the loss of their "property" (their enslaved workers). Most of the monies paid were not reinvested in Jamaica, but the sugar industry continued and white people continued to go to the island to buy estates that were being sold or to try their luck. Many of the newly freed blacks, with their own savings and sometimes with the help of the non-established religious denominations, set up their own smallholdings and communities.

On the whole Jamaica was moving ahead but in 1846 the British government passed legislation that had a huge and detrimental impact on the island's economy – the repeal of the Corn Laws ended the system of tariffs which protected its home-produced goods including sugar from its colonies. Further legislation throughout the 1850s dramatically opened up free trade with other nations outside the empire and, with no free labour to work the fields and with competition from cheaper slave-owning producers in Cuba and Brazil, the Jamaican economy went into dramatic decline.

Lord Olivier, governor between 1907 and 1915 but closely involved with Jamaica for decades after, first visited the island in 1897. A Fabian socialist, he wrote in 1936 that "If ever a community can be appropriately said to be ruined the white

Jamaica community was ruined in 1850. The mountain black people were not in the same sense ruined, but they were impoverished and their progress slackened." They had increased in number and their trade was diminished – well-to-do whites had left the island or were now in reduced circumstances so their custom was lost. Market prices and wages fell.

White people, particularly those who were Jamaican born, were in a tiny minority on the island in the mid-1860s. They lived with the background of slavery and rebellions against it. One rebellion, the Baptist War of 1831 in western Jamaica, was within living memory. On the island were a significant number of descendants of French families from the colony of Saint-Domingue (now Haiti) who could recall how the enslaved blacks and free people of colour had defeated the colonial power there. The "Black Hole of Calcutta" incident had taken place in India only nine years earlier. This was a time when an enlightened government that acknowledged the inequalities rife on the island could have taken steps to move the country forward. Instead, the Island's House of Assembly remained largely reactionary in its views towards black and coloured Jamaicans. In 1862 the equally reactionary and unsympathetic Edward John Eyre was appointed governor.

In 1865, in Jamaica's struggling economy, black labourers were increasingly unhappy with low wages and their treatment by employers and the governing establishment which seemed unable and unwilling to listen to grievances much less to sympathise or act. In the parish of St. Thomas, persistent maladministration of justice by the ruling whites – warrants for arrest were being used against blacks instead of simple court summonses – and the refusal of the Custos and the Governor to rectify the situation led to an inflamed local situation and an outbreak of violence. When reports arrived in Kingston of a disturbance involving killings in Morant Bay, the response from terrified whites was, almost inevitably, swift and severe. However, the actions of Governor Eyre, the army and its supporting forces (local militias and Maroons[1] living in the mountains of St. Thomas and Portland), were excessively and unnecessarily brutal. The resultant outcry in Britain led to the Jamaican-run government – its House of Assembly that had been in existence for over two hundred years – voting itself out of office. Eyre returned to Britain in disgrace.

Jamaica now, like most other British colonies, was to be run with significantly more input from London. A new governor was appointed, Sir John Peter Grant, who was at the end of a highly regarded career in India and considered a perceptive and strategic-minded colonial administrator. He was to do for Jamaica what no governor before him had done – he was to govern taking all of Jamaica's population into account.

Between 1866 and 1874, Grant put Jamaica's finances on a better footing, disestablished the church, reorganised the parishes, moved the capital from Spanish Town to Kingston, opened a Government Savings Bank and initiated an

[1] During the Spanish period (1494-1655), enslaved blacks who escaped their masters, formed the first Maroon communities in the mountains of Jamaica. Unable to defeat them, the British were forced to treaty, agreeing that they would control their own land. In return, however, the Maroons were to return escaped slaves to their owners. Despite their support to the British, they are held in high regard by Jamaican people because of the inability of the British army to defeat them and for their distinct culture.

important new irrigation project (the Rio Cobre system). In addition, he instituted an extensive public works programme that built new roads, bridges and public buildings including hospitals and elementary schools throughout the island. This extensive programme of reform and reorganisation is considered to have laid the foundations of modern Jamaica.[2]

Edward Austin Dodd's father, John Hugh Dodd, would participate in the projects of Governor Grant and his successors and Edward Austin would be born into a more peaceful and stable Jamaica than the one his father had known when he was young.

---

[2] Vincent John Marsala, *Sir John Peter Grant, Governor of Jamaica, 1866-1874* (Institute of Jamaica, 1972), 105

3 THE LIFE AND TIMES OF E. A. DODD

Family

Edward Austin Dodd – "Eddie" to his family – was born on 29 January 1882 in Port Antonio, a small town on the north-eastern coast of Jamaica, the main town of the parish of Portland.[3]

Eddie's father, John Hugh Dodd (1851-1896), was a commissioned surveyor and civil engineer in the Government's Public Works Department. He spent most of his life in Kingston, starting and ending his career there. In between the Kingston appointments, he was the Engineer in charge of the Eastern part of Jamaica. John Hugh had been born on the island to an English father and a Jamaican mother. His father, John, was from a long-established sheep-farming family who owned and leased land in Cumberland in northern England.[4]

Family tradition has it that John Dodd had come out to Jamaica in 1838.[5] He went to work on Cornwall estate in the parish of Westmoreland.[6] In 1848, John married Helen Mary

---

[3] In one of his articles Eddie wrote that he had lived in Port Antonio for a couple of years but, based on his father's career history and date and location of birth of his younger siblings, he must have spent the first seven or eight years of his life there.

[4] In Cumberland the Dodds leased some land from the Musgrave family but the connection, if any, between that family and that of Sir Anthony Musgrave who was Governor of Jamaica, 1877-1883, is unclear.

[5] They had been legally freed in 1834 but forced to serve a period of 'apprenticeship' of six years. Jamaica decided to end the 'apprenticeship' system two years early and other colonies followed suit.

[6] Cornwall had been owned by Matthew Gregory Lewis (1775-1818),

Josselyn whose paternal grandfather had immigrated to Jamaica in the late eighteenth century to Montego Bay where he married Mary Forbes née Sanders

John Dodd died a month after John Hugh's birth. Helen Mary remarried another Englishman who had gone out to Jamaica to work as a planter. Her new husband, Samuel Sharp Wortley, brought up her two children by John Dodd with their own. Wortley worked for several estate owners "with great success and to the oft acknowledged satisfaction of those who had entrusted him with the management of their properties"[7]. In the 1850s he took his family to the United States and tried farming there but returned to Jamaica where he was appointed the City Surveyor of Kingston. According to private family history, from the age of thirteen, John Hugh was "put to work" by Wortley who taught him the basics of surveying.[8]

John Hugh's first work experience was to help his stepfather in the reconstruction of the heart of commercial Kingston after the devastating fire of 1862 which destroyed at least thirty-five business premises in the prime commercial area and three wharves. He helped Samuel Sharp Wortley "in the reconstruction of Streets and Lanes of Kingston for which there was a Government grant of £18,000: [he was] employed in keeping [a] detailed statement of cost, measuring artificers work, and preparing plans and Sections."[9]

---

the author of the 1795 Gothic novel, *The Monk*, and had been willed to Lewis's sister, Fanny Lushington, whose family owned the property until the early twentieth century.

[7] *Colonial Standard*, 25 July 1878, 2.

[8] R. P. S. Dodd, *Windows of Opportunity*, 1986.

[9] The Institution of Civil Engineers: John Hugh Dodd application, 26 Apr

John Hugh must have been considered a capable aide for, in 1870, he became Assistant to the Government Surveyor, Thomas Harrison, and was indentured to him in 1871, being examined and qualified as a Commissioned Land Surveyor in June 1876.[10] A month later, probably feeling that he was now in a position to support a family, he married.

His wife, Sarah Johnstone, had been born in Demerara, British Guiana, where her father was the Health Officer for the port of Georgetown. Sarah's maternal grandmother was an Austin from a family that had lived in Barbados and British Guiana for several generations. Her maternal grandfather was William Edward Pierce from Jamaica.[11] The family were living in England in 1866 when Sarah's father died and her mother, in straitened circumstances, sent her to Jamaica to live with her Pierce family.

John Hugh Dodd and Sarah were married in St. Michael's Church, Kingston, by her uncle, the Reverend William Edward Pierce[12]. They had nine children over the next thirteen years. Their first three children, sons, were born in the house they bought in January 1877 in the parish covered by St Michael's, No. 5 Elletson Road, in Rae Town.

1884.

[10] Ibid.

[11] William E. Pierce, though born in Jamaica, spent fifty years of his life in Demerara. He returned home to Jamaica the year before he died. Source: *Monumental Inscriptions of Jamaica* by Philip Wright, 1966.

[12] Initially set up as an outreach chapel of the Kingston Parish Church. Eventually, it became an independent church serving the needs of the then middle-class community of Rae Town. Named after his father, William E. Pierce was Rector at St Michael's, 1868-1880.

In 1879, the Jamaica Railway Company was bought out by the Government and Valentine G. Bell, an experienced English civil engineer, was recruited by the Colonial Office and sent to the island. John Hugh Dodd was seconded to Bell for nine months, ascertaining the proposed routes of the Jamaica Railway extension lines from Old Harbour to Porus and from Spanish Town to Ewarton. At the end of this period, Bell wrote Dodd a reference which gained him an important job in the Public Works Department.[13]

In 1880, John Hugh was appointed Engineer Eastern District of Jamaica in 1880.[14] The appointment was based in Port Antonio so the Dodd family moved there from Kingston and Eddie was born in the town in 1882.[15]

Port Antonio

Until 1871, Port Antonio had been a small town in Portland. That year, the American merchant, Lorenzo Dow Baker, shipped a consignment of bananas from Port Antonio to Boston and, on the basis of the profits he made from the venture, moved his family to Jamaica and set up in the banana export business. In 1881 Lorenzo Dow Baker & Company shipped 30,000 stems of bananas.[16] By 1893/4, his Boston Fruit Company was shipping nearly three million

---

[13] *The Handbook of Jamaica for 1889-90* (Kingston: Government Printing Establishment, 1890).

[14] The National Archives, Kew, London: CO 137/499/31.

[15] Four more Dodd children were born there between 1883 and 1888, whilst a ninth and final child would be born in Kingston in 1890.

[16] Banana fruits grow in hanging clusters, also called a *bunch* or *stem*. The fruits grow in rows called *tiers* or *hands*. There can be as many as twenty fruits to a hand, and as many as twenty hands on a stem.

stems of bananas and five million coconuts.[17] The impact on Portland and the surrounding parishes was tremendous.

The Dodd family lived on the Titchfield peninsula. Eddie's oldest brother, John Hugh after their father [henceforward referred to as John Hugh II], attended Titchfield School in Port Antonio.[18] The school, originally set up during George III's reign, had been closed in 1855 but re-established in 1886 as a day school, no doubt to accommodate the children whose fathers were working in the booming banana economy.[19] This was just at the time when the older Dodd boys were ready to enter formal education. It is likely that Eddie and other brothers, when they reached an appropriate age, followed John Hugh to Titchfield. Outside of their formal education, Sarah Dodd, in the tradition of late nineteenth century middle class Victorian mothers, probably took responsibility for educating her children in the genteel arts... reading, painting and playing music.

At that time people derived a large part of their entertainment from reading. Before electricity was common, in the evenings, family members would gather round their dining table with kerosene [hurricane] lamps at its centre and read - books, magazines, and newspapers. (This was still the case in rural Jamaica where there was no electricity well into the 20th

---

[17] Bob Lyall, *The Tokens, Checks, Metallic Tickets, Passes, and Tallies of the British Caribbean & Bermuda* (The Token and Medal Society, 1988), 95-96.

[18] He also attended St. George's, York Castle and Potsdam. The Institution of Civil Engineers: John Hugh Dodd [II] application, 18 May 1905.

[19] *The Handbook of Jamaica for 1900* (Kingston: Government Printing Establishment, 1900), 329.

century.) In the days before the "wireless", magazines and newspapers were important sources of entertainment. Periodicals such as *Blackwoods*, *The Saturday Evening Post* and the *Atlantic Monthly* would have been staple reading fare for middle class families and were imported into Jamaica from Britain and the United States.[20]

Eddie and his siblings, however, were exposed to cultural influences that were not just British or American. Jamaican families like his usually had servants and most servants were Jamaicans of African heritage brought up on African songs and stories, related orally. The enslaved people from West Africa had brought with them fables about the character Anancy, who was sometimes a spider, sometimes a human, but always a cunning trickster. These stories were passed down through the generations and every Jamaican child would have heard stories about Anancy, whether told them by their grandmother, aunty, nurse, gardener or cook.[21] White, black and brown Jamaican children were equally enthralled by these songs and stories (and equally terrified by duppy stories).

Eddie's formal education would have exposed him to classical literature and help teach him how to think and how to write.

---

[20] *The Speaker, The Spectator, The Illustrated London News, Punch, The Strand Magazine* and *The Review of Reviews* were all taken by York Castle School. Source: *Ansell Hart's Monthly Comments*, Volume 6, http://archive.is/TfJS (Accessed: 20 April 2018).

[21] Anancy is the modern form of Anansi, the Ashanti word for "spider", and "Annancy" which was the spelling used in Jamaica until more recent times. Ashanti people are an ethnic group native to the Ashanti Region of modern-day Ghana (previously the British colony, The Gold Coast).

He would have read both the critically acclaimed and the popular writers of the here today and gone tomorrow variety. But when he had exhausted his books on the many long rainy days that occur in Portland, he would have visited the kitchen to listen to Jamaican stories, real and imaginary, relayed by the cook and the gardener, probably like his father and mother before him.[22]

Manchester

In 1890 the Dodd family returned to Kingston because John Hugh Dodd was appointed Engineer Central District and Irrigation Engineer for the important Rio Cobre project.

However, in 1892 when he was only 40 years old (and Eddie only ten), John Hugh was forced through ill health to take early retirement from government service. On the strength of recommendations from Valentine Bell, Director of Public Works, and James Henry Clark, the Government Medical Officer, the Governor agreed that John Hugh should be awarded an early pension. The pension was generous by the standards of the day but it would not have covered the costs of educating John Hugh's seven sons and two daughters. By chance, in January, the very same month that John Hugh was certified as being unfit to work, his uncle in England died, leaving most of his estate to his nephew.[23]

---

[22] The parish of Portland lies in the direct path of the prevailing northeast trade winds that bring rain, and its hilly terrain traps the winds and ensures almost daily rainfall. Source: Jamaica Information Service. http://jis.gov.jm/information/parish-profiles/parish-profiles-portland/ (Accessed: 29 April 2018).

[23] Will of Joseph Dodd, Gentleman, of Penrith, Cumberland, dated 11 February 1891.

Also in 1892, a pimento property, Lottery Pen in the parish of Manchester, was advertised in the daily newspaper, *The Gleaner*, for sale by Nunes & Co., Auctioneers. It comprised "a run of land of about 630 acres and is well subdivided by stone walls and wire fences. One field of common standing in pimento trees, the crop of pimento is from 300 to 400 bags.[24] The water tanks, barbecues and outbuilding are all in good order. The property will be sold with cost of cultivation … The Stock and Furniture will be sold at a valuation."[25]

Traditionally, properties used to rear cattle, horses, asses and mules were referred to as pens. The animals were sold mainly to estates and plantations where they were used to power mills and to transport goods and people. Some pens diversified and also produced pimento and/or coffee, cotton and logwood. Others were located on the fringes of towns and cities and functioned as residences of the wealthy.[26] Lottery was a diversified pen.

With his inheritance, John Hugh bought Lottery in the hills of southern Manchester. It was later renamed Glassonby, after the village in Cumberland, England, where John Hugh's father and uncle had lived. In Cumberland, Glassonby and its surrounds are characterised by dry stone walls bordering fields of sheep. Coincidentally, in Manchester, dry stone walls also characterise the landscape. But John Hugh did not buy Lottery for its stone walls; he bought it because of its location. High up, on an escarpment with views of the south coast of Jamaica in the distance, the breeze is strong and the

---

[24] A bag of coffee or pimento would weigh 100 lbs.

[25] *The Gleaner*, 1 January 1892, 6.

[26] B. W. Higman, *Jamaica Surveyed* (Institute of Jamaica, 1988), 197.

air cool and clear of any pollution. Ill with tuberculosis, John Hugh Dodd needed all the fresh air that Jamaica could provide.

Education - Potsdam and Pearman

With the Dodd family's move to Manchester, Eddie and most of his brothers were sent to be educated at Potsdam (later renamed Munro College), a school located high in the hills of the neighbouring parish of St. Elizabeth. Most schools in Jamaica at this time had been set up by the different religious denominations on the island. Potsdam, however, had been set up with legacies provided from the estates of Robert Hugh Munro, a local businessman and "gentleman of colour" who died in 1798, and Caleb Dickenson, believed to be Munro's nephew and also a successful businessman, who died in 1821.

The Munro and Dickenson Trust originally supported a number of schools in Manchester and St. Elizabeth.[27] The school that was to become Munro was first set up near the town of Black River in 1856 but relocated to a coffee property in the Santa Cruz mountain range of St. Elizabeth.[28] At a height of over 2,500 feet, it initially took on the name of the area in which it was located, Potsdam.[29] It was a small establishment and was largely run at a loss until 1871, when the trustees decided that the school would start to take paying

---

[27] *Blue Book for the Island of Jamaica 1866* (1867), S38-S39.

[28] Michael H. Elliott, *A History of Munro College and Hampton High School Located in Jamaica, in the parish of St. Elizabeth,* https://www.facebook.com/MunroHamptonInfrastructureFund/posts/714604505338655 (Accessed: 10 March 2018).

[29] Anti-German feeling during World War I occasioned the school's change of name to Munro, after its founder.

students, along the lines of English Grammar Schools of the time, to subsidise those who could not afford fees. It was from this point that, many decades after the deaths of Munro and Dickenson, the school was to develop a reputation for being one of the finest in the Caribbean. This was largely as a consequence of the leadership of the headmasters between 1875 and 1907; first the Reverend William Simms, and then the Reverend William Davis Pearman. Educated at Christ's College, Cambridge, Simms expanded the curriculum to include the Classics and English Literature. The reputation of the school grew and the number of students had doubled from 25 to 50 by the time Simms left to take up the headship at Jamaica College in St. Andrew in 1883. Pearman, Simms's replacement, was another Classics scholar, this time from St. Peter's College, Cambridge.

Potsdam took boarders and day students. As Lottery was several hours drive away along winding country roads, the Dodd boys would have boarded.

In 1893 John Hugh with his wife and second son, Henry "Harry" Jocelyn Dodd (1878-1946), travelled to the United States, to the Glockner Sanitorium in Colorado, where he hoped he might find a cure for his tuberculosis. Without antibiotics this was not to be. John Hugh returned to Jamaica and died at Lottery in 1896. Eddie was fourteen and a student boarding at Potsdam. His formal education and the development of his character, as was the norm in schools run on English public and grammar school lines, would now be in the care of the Reverend Pearman.

Pearman was a beloved headmaster, greatly mourned when he died suddenly, in 1907, after 24 years in post. His obituary in the Jamaican newspaper, *The Daily Telegraph,* described him as one of the island's "most popular and successful educators." It continued:

> *For nearly a quarter of a century, ...* [he] *has directed the work of the well known institution near Malvern; and all newspaper readers know how brilliant in its results that work has been. Year after year Potsdam boys have distinguished themselves in the Senior Cambridge examinations and in the competitions for the Jamaica scholarships ...* [and] *under Mr. Pearman, Potsdam was an educational centre of acknowledged excellence and honour. Not only was a high intellectual standard maintained, but the tone of the school was kept pure and lofty: with the result that the boys ... went out into the world with minds well stored and well trained, and also with gentlemanly instincts and ethical ideals that fitted them for entering on the serious battle of life with a reasonable hope of succeeding in the end.*

Pearman had had a brilliant career as a student and had edited publications of Cicero's writings that were published by Cambridge University Press; "But", his obituary in the Jamaican newspaper, *The Daily Telegraph,* continued, "he had none of the pedant's hauteur or affectation. He was essentially an amiable, humble, lovable man; and this accounted for his success as a teacher – his pupils were influenced alike by his polished intellect and his winsome, attractive character."[30]

Sarah Dodd pasted the newspaper cutting of this obituary

---

[30] *The Daily Telegraph*, 29 May 1907, 4.

into her bible, the only item in that volume that concerned a non-relative. In the circumstances, this was not surprising, for three of Sarah's sons, students at Potsdam, had won or were to win the Jamaica Scholarship. A widowed mother of nine children would have appreciated a headmaster who was good and kind as well as one who possessed the intellectual abilities that would help guide her sons. Although her father and two of her brothers took university degrees, we do not know how Sarah herself was educated.[31] However, her mother's financial privations and the academic achievements of her Pierce relatives would have left Sarah in no doubt of the importance of gaining a good education. Eddie and his younger brothers left a record of academic excellence. This was most probably the result of a combination of their being gifted along with an element of drive instilled in them by their widowed mother.

In 1899, at the end of Eddie's time at Potsdam when he was seventeen, he took the Cambridge Senior Examinations. He was in contention for the Jamaica Scholarship.

By the time the Dodd brothers were at school, Jamaican parents were able to hope that the very brightest of their children might be able to gain a university education. This would have to be abroad as there were no such institutions on the island.[32] The cost – tuition, accommodation and living expenses – of education abroad was beyond the pockets of all but the most wealthy so, to assist other hopefuls, various

---

[31] The brothers were James Pierce Johnstone M.D. (1859-1914) and Robert Johnstone C.M.G. (1861-1944).

[32] Two attempts to establish colleges of higher education, one in Spanish Town, the old capital of the island in St. Catherine in 1873, and one in the grounds of the Jamaica High School in St. Andrew in 1890, had both failed miserably.

scholarships, small and large, came into being.[33]

The Jamaica Scholarship, first awarded in 1881, was a substantial sum given by the Government to the top performing boy to allow him to study abroad.[34] In 1892, the Government decided that the award of £200 would be based on the result of the Cambridge Senior Local Examination.[35] This and the Rhodes scholarship, available to one Jamaican per year from 1904, were the most prestigious scholarships available to those who had gained their secondary education on the island. In addition, smaller Jamaica Scholarships of £10 and £15 were available to students while at school and several of the Dodd boys at Potsdam won a number of these.

In 1858, the University of Cambridge had established a Local Examinations Syndicate (now Cambridge Assessment) to administer examinations for school-leavers in Britain. The first colonial candidates were examined in 1863. The Cambridge Local Examinations were first held in Jamaica in 1882 and initially managed by the Institute of Jamaica. By 1887 an independent local committee had been set up and in 1898 there were 348 entries, of which 231 were successful.

The growth of the examination system in the empire was celebrated in a poem in the *Cambridge Review* in 1895.[36]

---

[33] The Gilchrist Educational Trust, 1869-1885, provided an annual scholarship of £100 per annum.

[34] In 1903, Miss Constance Pearman won and girls gained their own award from 1912.

[35] Previously, the award had been based on London Matriculation.

[36] J. P. C. Roach, *Public Examinations in England 1850-1900* (Cambridge University Press, 1971), 172. Claude McKay would write for the *Cambridge Review* when living in England in the 1920s.

Though Roman legions ruled the world,
Though Britain's thunderbolts are hurled
At monarchs in the Ashanti plains;
The Locals Syndicate preside
O'er realms more gloriously wide,
Broad as the sky are their domains
Black babes or yellow, brown or white,
Cram manuals from morn to night
No hue from culture now refrains;...

The comment on the ethnic makeup of the candidates was echoed the same year in Jamaica. *Gall's News Letter* published in Kingston reported that at the "Collegiate Hall" on the opening day of the Examinations, the candidates comprised "an interesting assemblage of young Jamaicans of every colour, creed and class".[37] (Proud as the newspaper was of the mix of the students, at this time these were boys from the mainly white and brown middle classes, not the mainly black working class. If there were black boys sitting the examination they would have been, in proportion to their numbers in society, a tiny minority.)

Eddie sat the examinations in Kingston with four other boys. Candidates who were examined in Kingston, rather than at their respective schools, were selected to do so – these boys and girls were considered to be the brightest students on the island. Eddie took papers in Arithmetic, Religious Knowledge, English, Latin, Greek, French, Spanish, Mathematics, and Applied Mathematics in December 1899 and was awarded Class I Honours overall, with distinctions in

---

[37] J. P. C. Roach, *Public Examinations in England 1850-1900* (Cambridge University Press, 1971), 175.

Latin and Mathematics. He came third in the island's ranking, and therefore in the Jamaica Scholarship competition, behind F. C. H. Powell, the winner, also of Potsdam, and J. C. Sharp of the Jamaica High School.[38] The fourth candidate was R. M. Murray who we shall meet later in this story.

Eddie had done well but not well enough. Without a scholarship his mother would not have been able to afford to send him abroad to university. Some boys, when they had not won a scholarship but had done well, would retake the examinations the following year. Eddie, coming third, may not have felt that it was worth it and he did not retake.

Professional training and early career

Having acquired an excellent secondary education but without the chance of going abroad to carry out further studies, Eddie probably spent some time considering what career he should pursue. His father had followed in his own step-father's footsteps and become a surveyor and engineer. Two of his elder brothers, John Hugh II and Joseph "Joe", also went into engineering and so did Eddie.

The earliest reference we have for this is in June 1907 when *The Gleaner* announced that "Mr. Dodd, assistant engineer at the railway… will go on three months' leave shortly…"[39] In July he left Port Morant in eastern Jamaica on the *S.S. Bella*. His profession on the ship's passenger list was listed as Civil Engineer; his home was Newport so he was, at that point, based at the family property, Glassonby, in Manchester. He was on his way to Montreal, Canada. It is possible that his

---

[38] *The Gleaner*, 14 April 1900, 3.
[39] *The Gleaner*, 4 June 1907, 4.

trip was to investigate accommodation and other matters relating to the arrival of his mother and some of his siblings who were to live in Montreal for a few years: Geoffrey, had won the Jamaica Scholarship and was to take up his university studies in the Autumn term of that year at McGill University and Helen was to embark on training to be a nurse at the Royal Victoria Hospital, affiliated with McGill.

An apprenticeship to become an engineer was a five year commitment. Between 1900, when Eddie left Potsdam, and 1907, when he had become a Civil Engineer, was sufficient time in which to serve an apprenticeship. With whom he served his apprenticeship is unknown. It is probable that his eldest brother, John Hugh II, with a rising career in the railway, would have taken on the responsibility for his training.

John Hugh II had followed in his father's footsteps, learning "on the job", with his first experience being gained while accompanying his father when he was surveying eastern Jamaica.[40] Like his father, John Hugh II then went to work for a senior engineering professional, Mr. Latham, Chief Engineer for Railway Extension, and pursued a career in the public works and the Jamaican railway for the next twenty odd years.

For the few years after 1907 it is unclear where Eddie's career in the railway took him in Jamaica. We know that in June 1908, he was appointed Junior Assistant to John Hugh II, the Railway's Engineer of Way and Works so was probably based in Kingston.[41] He was certainly in Kingston between 1910-

---

[40] The Institution of Civil Engineers: John Hugh Dodd [II] application, 18 May 1905.

1912 as he was welcomed onto the committee of the Kingston Athenaeum in April 1910 and served for two years when he retired from the committee on his "removal from Kingston."[42]

Marriage, children and later career

In June 1911, Eddie married Hilda Evelyn Sharp at the St. Andrew Parish Church. Hilda was the daughter of James Cunliffe Hicks Sharp. She was born in Kingston in 1887 while her father was off the island in Colon (then part of Colombia, now in Panama). At some point, James Sharp took his family from Jamaica to live in Costa Rica where he was managing a banana plantation owned by Minor Cooper Keith (1848-1929), the American businessman. In 1891, while working for Keith, Sharp died. Journeying into the interior of the country in order to inspect another banana property, he encountered heavy rains and flooding so fierce that railway bridges had been swept away. Despite being sixty miles from his destination, he determined to make his journey on foot. Two thirds of the way to the plantation, he passed through a forest where tree felling was taking place and was crushed by a tree that unexpectedly fell over and onto him. He was only 32.[43] His wife and children returned to Jamaica where they were supported by their large and close family of Sharps and Evelyns who lived in Clarendon and St. Catherine.[44]

---

[41] *Blue Book for the Island of Jamaica 1916-1917.*

[42] *Jamaica Times*, 27 April 1912, 21.

[43] *The Gleaner*, 24 December 1891.

[44] One of Hilda's uncles was Francis Greenidge Sharp, a planter in Clarendon whose Trout Hall estate was to become famous in Jamaica for Ugli Fruit and other citrus products. Another of Hilda's uncles was Thomas Hicks Sharp who became a well-known planter based in

It is not known how Eddie met Hilda. It may have been through tennis. Hilda's address when she got married was Arnold Road which was close to the St. Andrew Club where Eddie was a member. Few families in Jamaica will have been as keen practitioners of sport as the Dodd family. Eddie's father had played cricket for Portland Cricket Club and probably took part in other sports. His sons enthusiastically played and competed in tennis, fishing, shooting, riding, swimming, sailing and golf, often successfully. Eddie was no exception and, according to reports in *The Gleaner*, tennis was clearly his sport of choice. In 1910 he was the champion tennis player of the Railway Club (in Kingston) where both cricket and tennis were played.[45]

The Sharps were keen on tennis too. According to one member of the Sharp family: 'There wasn't a great population in that area [Chapelton] so everyone knew everyone! Everyone played tennis in those days. There was a tennis court at Trout Hall which was in top shape and actively used by the Clarendon families in those days and in fact was in use still when I was a child. Wonderful Sunday parties with sumptuous teas put on by my grandmother."[46]

Eddie and Hilda may also have met through mutual friends or neighbourly familiarity. Eddie's short story, *The Professor's John Crow*, might hold a clue. The characters, Christine and Dick, a young engineer, live next door to one another and

Clarendon and St Catherine, a member of the Legislative Council, and a leading light of the Jamaica Agricultural Society. *The Gleaner*, 22 March 1935, 3.

[45] *The Gleaner*, 12 December 1910.

[46] Josephine Meany (née Sharp), email to Rosie Dodd, 30 January 2018.

Dick is courting Christine. It is not unreasonable to imagine Eddie's story was inspired by real life.

However they met, Eddie and Hilda were living at Trewirgie, Ripon Road, near Cross Roads, by May 1912 when Hilda gave birth to Geoffrey Evelyn. In September 1913, Dorothy was born. At Trewirgie, Eddie and Hilda had their own tennis court and were within walking distance of the St. Andrew Club.

In April 1913, Eddie was living in the Chapelton area of Clarendon where he was most likely undertaking engineering work for the railway.[47] Work on the railway in the area involved the construction of a line through upper Clarendon from May Pen to Danks near Chapelton. Public pressure for this new line had begun in the early 1900s. The region was very fertile, produced large quantities of bananas and citrus, and farmers wanted a more efficient way of getting their crops to market. An area mainly of smaller rather than larger properties, the people wanted the train so that they could ship their produce and travel more easily. Proposals were discussed in the papers for years with a very specific route being proposed at meetings.[48] At last, in 1911, the Legislative Council approved the building of a branch railway line from May Pen up the valley of the Rio Minho through Suttons to Danks, near Chapelton, a distance of 13 miles. It was opened in September 1913.[49]

---

[47] Eddie lost an umbrella at the Educational Supply Company in Kingston and offered a reward if it were returned to him care of Chapelton Post Office. See: *The Gleaner*, 12 April 1913, 12.
[48] *Jamaica Times*, 18 February 1905, 7.
[49] The extension from Chapelton to Frankfield was not completed until

(If Eddie was involved with the construction of the line in 1913, he may well have taken part in the surveying of the line beforehand. Eddie may have met Hilda in Clarendon through professional or social acquaintance with Sharps or Evelyns at that time.)

Also in 1913, Eddie became a member of The Concrete Institute, London. In 1916, he was a Colonial Fellow of The Surveyors' Institution where John Hugh II was also a Colonial Fellow.[50] John Hugh II had become an Associate Member of the Institution of Civil Engineers in 1905, and a member of the Railway Signal Association in 1907. These professional qualifications would no doubt have served in John Hugh II's favour in his appointment as Engineer of Way and Works in 1908; Eddie would have been encouraged by his brother to follow suit where possible.

Interestingly, Eddie also became a member of the Jamaica Agricultural Society in 1915. Was this in relation to his work or had his wife's family encouraged him to consider a career change?.[51]

An early death

Although Eddie wrote very little that we know of after his

---

after the end of the First World War and another eight years had gone by.

[50] *List of Honorary Members, Members, Associate Members, Associates, Students, and Special Subscribers* (The Concrete Institute [later The Institution of Structural Engineers], September 1914), and *Transactions, Session 1917-1918, Vol. L.* (The Surveyors' Institution [later The Royal Institution of Chartered Surveyors], 1918.)

[51] *The Gleaner*, 19 February 1915

marriage and the birth of his two children, he did stay involved in literary matters. He was active in the Kingston Athenaeum on and off between 1910 and his death.[52] In 1910, at the age of 28, Eddie became a member of the committee. He may have been encouraged to join by his half-uncle, the Reverend Edward Jocelyn Wortley, who was also a member of the committee.[53] In the report of the 1910 AGM, Eddie was thanked for his donation of books to the library.[54] Two years later, he stood down from the committee owing to "his removal from Kingston." (We do not know precisely when he returned to Kingston but it was by 1915.) At the 1917 annual general meeting Eddie was elected to the post of Honorary Treasurer. Sadly, this would not be a post he was in for long. In the report of the Kingston Athenaeum's 1918 AGM, Eddie's death was described as "a distinct loss to the society" for he had taken "a keen interest in the affairs of the society, his fine literary taste being of great help to the committee in selecting books for the library."[55]

---

[52] He was also a member of the Institute, at one point supporting the nomination of J. L. Pietersz for Governor. Source: *The Gleaner*, 17 March 1917, 1. [*The Gleaner* prints 'T. A. Dodd' but we are certain this is a printer's error and the signee was indeed E. A. Dodd.]

[53] The Reverend Canon E. J. Wortley (1858-1928), was the son of Samuel Sharp Wortley and Eddie's grandmother, Helen Mary Wortley, widow of John Dodd. He was Rector at St. Andrew Parish Church, Canon of the Cathedral at Spanish Town, Chairman of the Board of Visitors for the Beckford and Smith's Free School. A director of Mico College and the Deaconess Home School for Girls (later St. Hugh's High School) amongst other offices held, he also founded The Wortley Home for Girls.

[54] *The Gleaner*, 13 April 1910, 3.

[55] *The Gleaner*, 11 April 1918, 13.

Edward Austin Dodd was only 35 when he died on 14 December 1917. He left his wife, Hilda, and two children, Geoffrey Evelyn, aged five, and Dorothy, aged four. His occupation on the death certificate is "engineer". A short obituary in *The Gleaner* stated that he was "late Junior Assistant Engineer of Ways and Works of the Jamaica Government Railway. The deceased gentleman has been ill for some time."[56] Like his engineer father, Eddie died of tuberculosis (a "tubercle of [the] lung"). The disease must have progressed quickly as he was healthy enough to have won a charity doubles tennis match at the St. Andrew Club on 7th June 1917.[57]

No obituary appears to have been published in the *Jamaica Times*. Perhaps it had been too long a time since his last published piece. Possibly Thomas MacDermot was preoccupied with other matters, such as the Great War. However, the relationship between the Dodd family and the owners of the newspaper, the Duries, endured. Seventeen years later, at the wedding ceremony of Eddie's daughter, Dorothy, in January 1935, one of the guests present was Mrs. Alice Durie, the widow of Walter Durie.[58]

The family kept his name alive – his brother Joe's son, born less than five months after Eddie's death, was named Edward.

---

[56] *The Gleaner*, 15 December 1917, 3.

[57] *The Gleaner*, 8 June 1917, 4.

[58] *The Gleaner*, 18 January 1935, 3.

4 THE CREATIVE WORKS OF E. A. DODD

The literary scene in early twentieth century Jamaica - Thomas MacDermot

Eddie Dodd's creative output dates from a time in Jamaica when literature and culture were coming to be highly valued. In the nineteenth century, Jamaican newspapers would occasionally carry a poem by a local contributor. In the last quarter of that century, improvements in education were to increase the potential number of writers eager to share their work. Larger towns with significant middle-class communities such as Brown's Town, Montego Bay and Spanish Town had a literary and/or improvement society of some kind. The societies aimed to create local libraries and hold regular public lectures on cultural, social and political topics.

In Kingston, there were two such societies: the Institute of Jamaica and the Kingston Athenaeum.[59] The Institute was established by the Governor in 1879 "for the encouragement of Literature, Science and Art".[60] It organised exhibits of Jamaican products at international exhibitions and, at its own annual exhibition of Art and Crafts, offered certificates and medals to contributors whose work was judged meritorious. It held regular lectures and its West India Reference Library contained an excellent collection of books and other material covering all aspects of Jamaica's heritage. The Kingston Athenaeum was founded in 1899 as an initiative of the Scots Kirk but was subsequently reconstituted on a wholly

---

[59] In the mid-nineteenth century the Colonial Literary Society, established in 1849, held regular lectures in Kingston.

[60] The Institute of Jamaica inherited the collection of the Royal Society of Arts and Agriculture which, a few years earlier, had found itself unable to continue owing to lack of funds and had donated its collections to the government.

independent basis. It was a literary society which had as its object "the promotion of the moral, intellectual and social welfare of its members."[61] It had a lending library for its subscribers, over the years based at different locations in Kingston such as above the Bee Hive Stores or the Cowen Music Room. Both the Institute and the Athenaeum held regular public lectures on a variety of subjects of a literary, social or political nature.

The *Jamaica Times* was a weekly paper published in Kingston and distributed island-wide. Published on Saturdays it always included an episode of a serialised story, often a short story and usually several poems. It had been established in 1898 by Walter Durie, its English owner and editor, who was ably assisted by a Jamaican, Thomas MacDermot. The latter had joined the paper before January 1900 which was when his name appeared on the editorial page as Assistant Editor. He would become Editor in September 1904.[62]

Fig. 2 Thomas Henry Macdermot

MacDermot's family had been Jamaicans for generations. His

[61] *The Handbook of Jamaica for 1923* (Kingston: Government Printing Establishment, 1923), 553.

[62] W. A. Roberts, *Six Great Jamaicans* (The Pioneer Press, 1951), 95.

father was a clergyman who had carried out his work at various locations around the island. The family was closely connected to that of the Reverend Dr. William Clarke Murray, the well-known headmaster of York Castle School, where MacDermot received some of his education. Dr. Murray's wife was MacDermot's aunt. (A sister of his mother, they were born Ruttys.) MacDermot's own sister would marry her first cousin, Murray's son, Elias, and MacDermot would, on occasion, reside with his sister and brother-in-law at their home, The Lodge, Arnold Road, St. Andrew.[63]

At the *Jamaica Times,* whether as Assistant or Editor, Thomas MacDermot shouldered a great burden of the editorial work. As 'The Celt', he regularly wrote the paper's literary column. At a meeting with the writer Walter Adolphe Roberts in 1903, MacDermot complimented Roberts on his choice of local themes for his poetry saying that "it was the duty of rising talents to help create a Jamaican literature." Roberts, the first Jamaican to promote self-government for the island, felt that MacDermot was "keenly nationalistic" whose ideal was "Jamaica within the empire, but Jamaica as a recognised entity."[64] Whatever his political views, MacDermot certainly worked tirelessly to promote and support Jamaican writers. The themes in the short stories that he published – relations between Jamaican classes, stories about Jamaican peasants and folk culture – laid the ground for later writers.[65]

---

[63] Dr Murray's daughter, Kathleen, an inspirational and loved teacher at St. Hugh's Preparatory School, Tom Redcam Drive, Kingston, 1940s-1970s, was born at The Lodge, Arnold Road. Miss Kathleen Murray taught this writer to read.

[64] W. A. Roberts, *Six Great Jamaicans* (The Pioneer Press, 1951), 92.

[65] Leah Reade Rosenberg, *Nationalism and the Formation of Caribbean*

MacDermot's own poems and short stories were published under the pseudonym 'Tom Redcam', MacDermot spelt backwards. His work is dated and largely forgotten, but his name lives on in Kingston where the St. Andrew Parish Library on Tom Redcam Drive is known as the "Tom Redcam Library".

The daily paper, *The Gleaner*, also published literary contributions from its readers. Its annual Christmas Short Story Competition usually attracted a good number of entries, not least because it offered a cash prize as well as the prestige of the winning entry being published in the paper. Respect for MacDermot was such that, despite being from a rival paper, he was often called upon to judge the competition.

Poems

From September 1902 to July 1906, eighteen of Eddie Dodd's poems were published in *The Gleaner* or in the *Jamaica Times*, mainly in the latter. Unusually, one, *New Year's Eve*, was published with slightly different wording in both papers. The poem, *Night*, containing imagery of Jamaican fireflies, is Eddie's first recorded published work and was carried in the 13 September 1902 edition of the *Jamaica Times*. *Night* was printed on the pages that carried the editorial columns which is where MacDermot's own poems and those of writers he admired, such as Walter Adolphe Roberts and Lena Kent, were usually printed. Eddie was then only 20 years old.

That year, in December, Eddie shared the first prize for the *Jamaica Times* Christmas 'Poem on Jamaica' competition with *The Voice of the Purple Isle.* (The other winner was C. P. O'R. de

Montagnac, who under the pseudonym Zephyrus submitted *The Cocoanut Tree*.) MacDermot did not think much of most of the entries sent in commenting that only two, the prize winners, "were at all passable." *The Voice of the Purple Isle*, MacDermot felt was:

> *too irregular in construction; but displays a strong and promising power of poetic conception. The writer if he will study good models and learn to 'cut' and 'file' has that within him which may take him no small distance as a poet.*[66]

Eddie's poems are written in the lyric style, the dominant genre of the time, with simple meter and stanza forms, rhymes and rhythms. Unsurprisingly, for a young man in his early twenties who was presumably influenced by the Romantic and Victorian poets, a number of the poems relate to romantic love; many are set in the evening or night-time. Eddie used imagery to enhance and impart an atmospheric portrayal of this period of the day in a tropical climate – a time to relax in the cool and the dark, listening to the sounds of the natural world, to contemplate the events of the hot day just over and the one to come.

Eddie references the Jamaican natural world with the "flickering fireflies" which are "the jewels" worn by night that it "may lovelier seem". In *Evening*, he describes the "Bell Birds" with their ringing "Evening Call". Eddie's Bell Bird may well be the Tinkling Grackle which got its local name, Cling-Cling, from the sound that used to be made on an estate by the striking of a piece of metal against the iron rim

---

[66] *Jamaica Times*, 20 December 1902, 10.

of a suspended disused cartwheel. This signified the time that field gangs could knock off work and matched the notes of the Grackle.[67]

Some Ghosts is also set at night but not in pastoral south Manchester, rather in the capital city in an area where young people enjoyed promenading. One night in Kingston, Eddie appears to have seen the results of "a machine for making ghosts of curious colours and varied in shape". The poem is inspired by this sight and is humorous as well as curious and slightly unsettling. It is possibly Eddie's most Jamaican poem in that it relates to life in Kingston and Jamaican duppy culture.

Ariadne's Song and *Russia, A Prayer* are stylistically different in that they are written in the voice of another, Ariadne herself, and a Russian. *Russia, A Prayer* was published in 1906, after the Russo-Japanese war of 1904-1905 and during the Russian Revolution of 1905-1907, a time of great suffering for the people of Russia and, especially, its soldiers. Eddie empathises with Ariadne abandoned by Theseus on her Greek isle, and with the Russian people in what appear to be hopeless situations. Residents of small countries at the mercy of great powers have an interest in following significant happenings elsewhere in the world and Jamaican papers provided excellent coverage of foreign news. Eddie's older brother, Harry, had fought in the Boer War so it is very likely that he and the well-read Dodd family would have been attuned to international politics and accounts of wars across the globe.

---

[67] Source: May Jeffrey-Smith, *Bird-Watching in Jamaica* (The Pioneer Press, 1956), 79-80.

In May 1903, a poem of Eddie's introduced the readers of the *Jamaica Times* to his views on writing. *To the minor authors of to-day. A tribute to Writers like Merriman, Bret Harte, Mary Johnson* [sic] *etc.* referred to the authors, Hugh Stowell Scott, pseudonym Henry Seton Merriman (1862-1903), Francis Bret Harte (1836-1902), and Mary Johnston (1870-1936). One stanza hinted at how Eddie would later approach the writing of his stories:

Not always writ in Classic English,
Proper period, ponderous style;
But wrought in simple words you give us
Some new story just to pass the while.

Literary columns

In June 1903, when he was 21, writing under the pseudonym E. Snod, Eddie started to write columns for the *Jamaica Times* in which he recommended literary and other works to its readers. In his first column, he included a section on the art of letter writing, extracted from an American magazine, which suggests his attitude towards writing:

The letters need not be long, but they should be neat, correct and attractive, and they should say something and say it out of the routine.[68]

MacDermot may have seen E. A. Dodd, a bright young man, twelve years younger than himself, with opinions on literature, as someone who could write a regular column and ease the burden from the editor's shoulders. Eddie was to write only a few columns, no doubt owing to the pressure of

---

[68] *Jamaica Times*, 6 June 1903, 14.

work.[69] The literary columns in the papers usually contained recommendations. Eddie suggested writers from E. F. Benson to Euripides. He also expressed opinions as to how and what to write; opinions that clearly chimed with MacDermot's beliefs.

On 31 October, Eddie's column was devoted to Bret Harte, one of the "minor authors" to whom he had paid tribute in his poem. Harte's poems and short works of fiction featuring miners, gamblers, and other romantic figures of the California Gold Rush captivated Eddie. He liked the romance, humour, and patriotism of the stories, and enjoyed encountering Harte's characters when they reappeared in different tales. He felt that the poems were "for the most part what any 'fellow' can understand" and the "short and very realistic" stories, above all, had "charm and originality."[70]

His column of 27 June 1903 followed on from his first column and also concerns the art of writing. In essence, he sets out his approach to what constitutes good work that will stand the test of time:

> *It can in no way be doubted that there are many authors of to-day, whose books do a lot of good, that everywhere in magazine and novel, we meet with good wholesome matter, but do we meet with much that will live beyond its own generation? Of course the answer must be no, for putting aside the very few great things written that can suit mankind in all ages, the only things that can live are true and faithful descriptions of people and creatures of current life, and this is what should be noted carefully, — any true*

---

[69] *Jamaica Times*: 6 June, 27 June, 12 September, 31 October 1903.
[70] *Jamaica Times*, 31 October 1903, 8.

account of the manners of the people about you, their speech, their homes, the town or country you dwell in, will be of great value fifty years hence, and of much more two hundred years after. 'Kim,' which is the best of Kipling's novels, will certainly go down to posterity, but this is due to the wonderful way in which the mystery, and glamour of the East is brought out; to its descriptions and true feeling of life, but not to its plot. There are plenty of people in Jamaica doubtless, who would like to do something in a literary way, and who strive to write stories and poems after the magazine style, but whose efforts generally end in nothing, or nothing that is good. Well then, instead of copying mediocre writers, let them sit down and write[,] be it ever so poor, a true story of their life, their customs, dress, country and people, and they will have written something, the value of which will be priceless in years to come. And even today, its value will be greater than their weak attempts at original writing.[71]

Eddie had praised *minor* authors in verse; here he warned against copying *mediocre* writers. If Jamaican authors wrote about what they knew – Jamaican life, culture and people – then their works, even if not of much literary merit, would have lasting historic and cultural value.

Two weeks later, a *Jamaica Times* editorial (no doubt written by MacDermot) endorsed Eddie's approach:

E. SNOD in our Literary Column, June 27th, gave some excellent advice to young authors. We wish for their own sakes, and for the sakes of busy Editors they would

---

[71] *Jamaica Times*, 27 June 1903, 16.

take heed to his words. In nine cases out of eleven the young writer sets about writing his story, or poem, or drama, or sketch, about circumstances, and scenes, and people, with which or with whom he has no direct acquaintance whatever, and thereby authors ab initio are placed at a great disadvantage[;] they make it a foregone conclusion that they will imitate a picture of reality, and not paint the picture from reality itself.

They assign themselves to those who only know to paint and to draw from copies, who must wait patiently till some one else has looked into Nature's eyes, or tumbled her tossing locks, and reduced their impressions of her beauty, her energy, her [c]harm to words; they must wait on this, ere they can say anything; and when their say does come, it is apt to wear the difference that always yawns between the most finished artificial flower, and the humblest of natural ones. No doubt it is more difficult at first to learn that secret of reading Nature for ourselves, and in our own way of interpreting human problems and intricacies, but, once learned, we never again imitate consciously. It is the best cure for that affectation, that morbid sensitiveness, that swelling conceit that the bad fairies give with the glories and charms of the literary temperament. It is a temperament that more than all, needs the cool steady strong calm of nature; that needs, more than all others, to be face to face with truth, and reality, for, least of all temperaments, can it be helped by men and women, their conventions, and their artificialities.[72]

Eddie appreciated Bret Harte's stories for what they taught

---

[72] *Jamaica Times,* 11 July 1903, 13.

him about the lives of characters living in the American West and it is this, rather than his literary style, that continues to give Harte's work significance. Later, he was to follow the adventures of one character in several stories in a collection of his own.

After 1903, Eddie did not continue his literary column though a few more of his poems were published that year and in the next two years. Most of his creative time during 1904 was to be spent working on his own short stories which would have strong Jamaican themes. Like Bret Harte in America, the intensely local nature of the stories was to help to give Eddie his small place in the history of early Jamaican literature.

Thomas MacDermot was to give Eddie his opportunity.

Short Stories

Maroon Medicine – four short stories

In October 1903, the *Jamaica Times* published the first book in a literary project of MacDermot's.[73] *The All Jamaica Library* series, whether poetry, fiction, history or essays, was to be written by Jamaicans, about Jamaican subjects, and sold at a price so small as to be affordable to most Jamaicans.

The first volume printed was a novel by MacDermot (writing as Tom Redcam), *Becka's Buckra Baby*. On the day of its

---

[73] That month, the *Jamaica Times* also announced that the second volume in the series was to be entitled *Jordon and Some Other Jamaicans*. See: *Jamaica Times*, 24 October 1903, 13. In 1951, W. A. Roberts's *Biographical Sketches of Six Great Jamaicans*, Pioneer Press, 1951, included a chapter on Edward Jordon.

publication, the *Jamaica Times* noted that the Governor had ordered "the entire Series of the *All Jamaica Library*", a significant show of support for the venture. Four months later, an announcement was made on the editorial page that the second volume of *The All Jamaican* [sic] *Library* was now going to be a collection of short stories with the all-important Jamaican motif. The notice emphasised that the book was going to be by a new writer:

> *a young Jamaican not yet very widely known to readers here, but whose ability has been evinced by several bits of very graceful and beautiful verse in our columns and those of the Gleaner.*

> *He writes under the name E. SNOD, and after reading the forthcoming volume of his work we think Jamaicans will be anxious to see more from his pen.*

The book was to be entitled *Maroon Medicine and other Stories* to include *The Red Cock, Rum and Water,* and *The Country of the Dudes.*[74] In May 1905, *Maroon Medicine,* featuring the eponymous title story, *The Red Cock, Paccy Rum,* and *The Courting of the Dudes,* was published.

MacDermot laid out his philosophy behind *The All Jamaica Library* in his review of *Maroon Medicine.* With the very low prices being charged per volume, the Library was not a venture expected to make a profit with there being "little prospect for a long time at least" that it would become a paying concern. The piece indicated that the authors were not being paid for their works. Instead, they were "lending us the aid of their pens... generous enough to support us loyally in

---

[74] *Jamaica Times,* 6 February 1904, 12.

this position" and that if a "pecuniary profit" were to be made it would be a "happy issue from all our afflictions." MacDermot explained:

> *We have confidence that though latent there is a great deal of patriotism in Jamaica, a great deal of unity of feeling and wholesome genuine pride in the achievements of our Island's sons and daughters, without any sectional considerations as to the particular class or colour that they belong to. We say that we have confidence in the existence of such feelings, and that they need only to be properly stimulated and aroused. The day will come when all Jamaicans will have learnt the lesson of unity and of feeling, of practical patriotism, and of the patriotism of sentiment. When our interest in our history will be living and inspiring; when, in the lovely scenery or our Island Home, in her quaint corners of habit and custom, and in her legends and folk lore, we will take the interest that is natural and proper.*
>
> *Thoughts and ideas of this kind are behind the venture of "The All Jamaica Library" as they are behind others of our enterprises as a Business and a Paper.*[75]

The All Jamaica Library was clearly an idealistic project based on patriotism. Although we do not know Eddie's political views, it is likely that they were not dissimilar to MacDermot's. They certainly both wanted the development of Jamaica and its writing.

Maroon Medicine was well received by *The Gleaner*, which carried a review entitled "An Amusing Little Work". The

---

[75] *Jamaica Times*, 8 July 1905, 12-13.

reviewer felt that:

> *The style in which these stories are written makes easy reading and the writer has a gift of quiet humour... Much of the dialogue is given in dialect and the writer shows himself a good observer of the peculiarities of the peasant class... It is a readable publication, and we shall await the publication of the third number of the "All Jamaica Library" with interest.*[76]

MacDermot also appreciated Eddie's work, writing:

> *"Maroon Medicine" by E. SNOD portrays the lighter side of our pleasant life.*[77] *It is we think ill-natured at no single part, but it does not fail to satirize with effect some of the weaknesses, amiable or otherwise that our Island flesh is heir to. The use of the dialect is yet in that state in which English Spelling was in the days of CHAUCER and before; there has not as yet been established any standard manner of spelling it, or of making use of its idioms. Every writer doeth as seemeth to him best. E. SNOD we think handles it with both ability and weight. The reader feels that the author is writing of things that he has both seen and studied. "Maroon Medicine" contains good work, and we are gratified to place it in our Library.*[78]

In his stories, Eddie carried out the advice he had given writers in June 1903 when he advised them to write "true and faithful descriptions of people... [their] manners..., their

---

[76] *The Gleaner*, 29 July 1905, 8-9.

[77] It is likely that this is a printer's error and that MacDermot meant 'peasant', not 'pleasant'.

[78] *Jamaica Times*, 8 July 1905, 12-13.

speech, their homes, the town or country you dwell in." He had spent most of his formative years in the parishes of Manchester and St. Elizabeth and it shows in the places and names he used in his tales. Mr. Watson of the stories *Maroon Medicine, Red Cock,* and *Paccy Rum,* lives in the Manchester Hills, travels to Alligator Pond, Mile Gully, Williamsfield, amongst other places; all familiar to Eddie. Mr. Watson may owe his name to Watson's Hill that lies between Spur Tree and Alligator Pond. Eddie's descriptions of a police station and police operations suggest close knowledge of the workings of the police force. While he was writing *Maroon Medicine*, his brother, Harry, was a Sub-Inspector of Police and Eddie is likely to have either visited him at his place of work or listened closely to his descriptions about how police stations were run.

Leah Reade Rosenberg says that *Maroon Medicine* continued in "the tradition of comic folk literature" that the *Jamaica Times* and other papers were publishing.[79] In the preface to his book, Eddie does indeed suggest that he is emphasising the lighter side of life in Jamaica:

> *I have in no way touched upon the Social Problems[,] I might say Problem, – which, as a rule, engross the attention of writers who deal with life in Tropical Countries. On the contrary, I have avoided all such deep questions, and have attempted merely to portray the lighter and more pleasant side of the labouring class in the hills. The stories, indeed, are scarcely more than sketches, but sketches, from life, and as such may have some value.*

---

[79] *Nationalism and the Formation of Caribbean Literature by* Leah Reade Rosenberg (Palgrave Macmillan US, 2007), 51.

I have tried to instil into this little book, the spirit, so gay and careless of the people I have encountered, and their simple cuteness.[80] Mr. Watson, however, is hardly an ordinary type, and has been made up from two or three characters. Some people may object to the two love letters in the story, "The Courting of the Dudes," as being too well expressed and civilized, but it may be remarked that they were composed very much after the manner and matter of two or three letters that had been actually written and which I had the good fortune to read.

Kenneth Ramchand, commenting on *Maroon Medicine*, emphasized the importance of humour to West Indian culture, and pointed out other significant aspects of the book:

It is true that [the author] *does not tackle poverty, race or colour, with the passion and directness of later practitioners. But comedy and humour are also characteristic elements in the West Indian short story, and this portrayal of "the lighter and more pleasant side of the labouring class in the hills" does not only stand at the start of that tradition at its most pointed; it also has another kind of social awareness. It poses already, in the figure of Mr. Green* [in The Courting of the Dudes], *the crucial question of cultural mimicry. The earthy Mr. Watson* [in the other three stories], *immersed in place and intimate with people, getting around the Law and practicing alternative skills, comes over as a more native option than Mr. Green.[81]*

---

[80] Here, and in 1905, "cuteness" probably meant charm and appeal.

[81] Kenneth Ramchand: *The West Indian Short Story* (Journal of Caribbean Literatures, Vol. 1, No. 1 (Spring 1997), 21-33.

This issue of mimicry or mockery would be addressed by a contemporary critic a few years later with the publication of Eddie's story, *Farder Matney's Pigs*.

Maroon Medicine has been of interest to students of early Jamaican literature for two main reasons. First, the three stories about the clever and cunning trickster, Mr. Watson, are the first in Jamaican literature that feature someone with Anancy-style character traits who is a human being, not a shape-shifting spider. At the turn of the century, some writers and observers of Jamaican folk culture, were becoming interested in the stories of Anancy.[82] Eddie would have

---

[82] In 1899, Aston W. Gardner published *A Selection of Anancy Stories* by Wona, a pseudonym for Una Jeffrey-Smith, one of a large number of daughters of a family from Spanish Town, St. Catherine. At that time, Jeffrey-Smith was probably a teacher at the Deaconess High School (later St. Hilda's High School) in Brown's Town, St. Ann. A few years later, she would be its Headmistress and an instigator behind the establishment in the town of a branch library of the Institute of Jamaica. (Source: *The Gleaner*, 4 October 1911, 10.) Also in 1899, *Annancy Stories* was published in New York. This was a sumptuous book, written and lavishly illustrated by the British-American illustrator, Pamela Colman Smith, who had spent part of her youth in Jamaica. A significant and lasting contribution to the preservation of Jamaica's heritage was made by Walter Jekyll, an English intellectual living in the Blue Mountains who loved walking. Jekyll, an ex-clergyman, music teacher and Fabian socialist, went to Jamaica in 1894 and spent years collecting Anancy stories, songs and verses. These were published in 1907 in *Jamaican Song and Story* by The Folklore Society, London. (It is thought that Robert Louis Stevenson, who was a friend of Jekyll's, may have borrowed the name for his book, *The Strange Case of Dr Jekyll and Mr Hyde*. His sister was the gardener, Gertrude Jekyll.) In the 1966 Dover reprint, Louise Bennett, Jamaica's important folklorist paid tribute to Jekyll's work – she had

known Anancy stories from his childhood. However, it is more likely that, as he wrote in his preface, his stories were "sketches, from life", based on people he knew or incidents he had heard of. Whatever influenced him, in Mr Watson he created a human character who displayed Anancy's scheming ways and is a recognisable Jamaican personality.

A second reason for interest in *Maroon Medicine* is that it is the earliest book of fiction published in Jamaica that realistically employs Jamaican dialect. It has also been referenced as the earliest printed source for a number of Jamaican words and phrases.[83]

The first collection of short stories to feature Jamaican dialect was published in 1899 in London.[84] *Negro Nobodies* by Noel de Montagnac, an occasional contributor to *The Gleaner*, contained stories written in standard English with speech in English and in patois. De Montagnac was a Jamaican but much of his speech in dialect in the book is unconvincing. *The Gleaner* reviewer thought that it had been anglicised because the English publisher would have considered the language, as originally written, "too unintelligible" for its main market.[85]

In the early twentieth century, dialect in print in Jamaica was rare. Occasionally, poems such as *Done in Dialect*, were

forgotten many of the stories and songs she had heard in her childhood until she read *Jamaican Song and Story*.

[83] F. G. Cassidy and R. B. Le Page, *A Dictionary of Jamaican English* (University of the West Indies Press, 1967 and other editions).

[84] Noel de Montagnac, *Negro Nobodies* (T. Fisher Unwin, London, 1899).

[85] *The Gleaner*, 21 November 1899, 4.

published.[86] The patois was often not well reproduced and the tone of poems patronising. Many people in the early twentieth century looked down on "Negro talk" and "old-time sayings".[87] Publishers preferred standard English in the main body of a work but they did encourage the use of patois when they felt it appropriate and were even critical of unsuccessful efforts, as with de Montagnac's stories. The edict of *The Gleaner* in 1905 regarding its Christmas competition rather sums up the attitude. Competitors would not win unless they had a good command of English grammar and spelling and the use of dialect was acceptable but not if the story was nothing but dialect from beginning to end:

> *It may be clever, but it is quite unreadable to any outside a very narrow circle… there must be breathing spaces of pure and appropriately shaded English, or, else, the attempt to plunge through the story is like getting through a very thick and thorny hedge*[88]

The publication of *Negro Nobodies* prompted a call by *The Gleaner* reviewer for more writing about the people of the West Indies:

> *For many years we have been watching for a writer who will do for the West Indies what RUDYARD KIPLING has done for the East. Practically nothing is known abroad regarding the real life of the people of this region, and yet it is one rich in the outward elements of*

---

[86] *Jamaica Times*, 3 January 1903, 2, and 24 January 1903, 18.

[87] Philip Sherlock, *The Living Roots* in *Jamaican Song and Story* by Walter Jekyll (Dover edition, 1966), viii.

[88] *The Gleaner*, 23 December 1899, 11.

romance and throbbing with human interest and the passionate factors of life.[89]

Six years later, in 1905, two books were published that tried to do what *The Gleaner* reviewer had called for – Eddie Dodd's *Maroon Medicine* in Jamaica, and, more than a thousand miles away, *Negro Humour* by J. Graham Cruickshank in British Guiana.[90]

Cruickshank was born in British Guiana in 1877 and educated in Scotland. He lived and worked in British Guiana for nearly five decades, from 1896 until his death in 1944, probably in government service in Georgetown. He developed an interest in collecting and preserving the dialect and stories of "old time Negroes", and as well as *Negro Humour*, published *Black Talk, Being Notes on Negro Dialect in British Guiana, with (inevitably) a Chapter on Barbados* in 1916. He has been referred to as "the most important chronicler of early-twentieth century [Guyanese Creole]… a close and accurate observer of the language and culture of the "ordinary people." "[91]

Negro Humour was a collection of stories based on incidents that Cruickshank had observed. According to the author's introductory note, most of the stories had been published before in the local newspapers, *The Argosy* and *The Daily Chronicle*. He felt that:

---

[89] *The Gleaner*, 21 November 1899, 4.

[90] J. Graham Cruickshank, *Negro Humour: Being Sketches in a Market, on the Road, and at my Back Door* ("The Argosy" Company, Demerara, 1905).

[91] John R. Rickford, *Dimensions of a Creole Continuum: History, Texts & Linguistic Analysis of Guyanese Creole* (Stanford University Press, 1987), 112.

For some such sort of wayside sketches, — but deeper, —
the West Indies seem to offer rather neglected opportunity.
We have a unique people: worth study, with sympathy,
and with reference emphatically to their past: a magnificent
historical and geographical background.

The approach and style of writing of Cruickshank and Eddie is remarkably similar. They used standard English with speech in English and in patois and, unlike de Montagnac, they mainly focussed, lightly, on the humorous. Through listening, understanding and using dialect well they were better able to convey their understanding of the people they were interested in and wanted to write about.

As with the other titles in *The All Jamaica Library* series, the *Jamaica Times* publicised *Maroon Medicine* through advertisements, some illustrated, in its pages. Eddie may have produced these illustrations – see Figures 4 and 6 – for they are not dissimilar in style to others that he contributed to a later series of his writing in the *Jamaica Times*.

Fig. 3 Advertisement for *Maroon Medicine*, 12 August 1905

Fig. 4 Advertisement for *Maroon Medicine*, 05 August 1905

The large local store, Hylton's Times Stores, thought that *The All Jamaica Library* series might appeal to foreign visitors to Jamaica. As well as picture books and guides to the island, *Becka's Buckra Baby* ("A clever sketch of local life") and *Maroon Medicine* ("Another sketch dealing with a different phase of Jamaican life") were included in the store's advertisements listing *Books for Tourists* in *The Gleaner,* and their good value emphasized.[92]

Sadly, *The All Jamaica Library* series was not, overall, a success and although the *Jamaica Times* intended the series to cover twelve titles, only four books were published.[93] The first,

---

[92] *The Gleaner*, 29 January 1906, 12.

[93] *Jamaica Times*, 26 September 1903, 10.

Becka's Buckra Baby by Tom Redcam, came out in 1903, and the last, *One Brown Girl And –*, also by Redcam, in 1909. *Becka's Buckra Baby* ran to at least three editions but the 1907 earthquake and subsequent fire – although it inspired the story in the third book – likely caused stocks of the first two titles to be damaged or destroyed. In any case the quality of the writing in the series, with the exception of *Maroon Medicine*, left something to be desired. Walter Adolphe Roberts did not consider Redcam's prose and dialogue to be his forte[94] and Mervyn Morris thinks Redcam's writing was often rather too morally earnest and dull.[95] Turning a profit was not a principal aim of the series but financial success would certainly have strengthened its future prospects.

In 1907, in a short article in the *Jamaica Times* doubtless written by MacDermot, the lack of financial success of *The All Jamaica Library* is alluded to:

> *It is a thousand pities that there is not more pride and interest in our own local writers like L.A.R., LENA KENT, C.M.G., or EVA R. NICHOLAS, not to mention the male singers like W.A.R. and E. SNOD, "Mandeville," etc. In other countries talent of the kind is valued and encouraged, and toward that things are slowly changing in Jamaica. The day is not far distant, we hope when local publications will no longer be a certain monetary loss.*[96]

---

[94] W. Adolphe Roberts, *Six Great Jamaicans* (The Pioneer Press, 1951), 101.

[95] Mervyn Morris, *The All Jamaica Library* in *Jamaica Journal* Vol. 6 No. 1 (Institute of Jamaica, March 1972), 49.

[96] *Jamaica Times*, 20 July 1907, 10.

The piece also, however briefly, affirmed MacDermot's admiration for Eddie's work and the distance he had travelled since his success in the 1902 Christmas poem competition.

Lorita

In the same year that *Maroon Medicine* with its humorous stories was published, Eddie won *The Gleaner's Local Christmas Prize Story Competition* from a field of 58 entries.[97] *The Gleaner* offered a substantial prize for its Christmas Story Competition. In 1905 it was £2 2s (two guineas) for "the best original story not to exceed 4,400 words, or four columns of the GLEANER. The plot must be laid in Jamaica and at least one of the characters must be Jamaican. The story may be based on fact or fiction."[98]

Eddie's prize winning entry, *Lorita*, was quite different in subject matter and style from the four comic stories published in *Maroon Medicine*. It is an example of Eddie's work that shows kind and imaginative sensibilities.

Thomas MacDermot had been the competition judge the year before and was so again in 1905. Stories entered into the competition were presented to the judge without the authors' names. Eddie would have been aware that it was very likely that MacDermot would judge the competition and may have chosen this completely different theme for his entry to give himself the best possible chance of not being recognised.

In his report, MacDermot felt that most of the writers of the

---

[97] Eddie had also entered the Gleaner's Christmas Story competition in 1904. See the discussion below regarding *Farder Matney's Pigs*.

[98] *The Gleaner*, 16 December 1905, 34.

1905 entries, despite having the power "of conceiving the central idea", were "careless about perfecting the minor but necessary part of working out details" and of making the language "clear, graceful and attractive." Six stories stood out for him; one indeed ranked high but was "outclassed by one or two others, and in living power by" *Lorita*. The published adjudication states:

> *Taking everything into consideration, this is the story that I think most deserves the prize in the present competition; and I therefore have pleasure in recommending it for that distinction. It is not as exciting as some of the others, it does not show as much power in characterisation as is displayed in part of No. 19, and it has not as a whole the easy grace in language that was noticed in No. 48. But the story is sufficiently interesting; it is clearly thought out, displays feeling and artistic insight, good, and at times marked literary ability, and a healthy tone, clean and honest. The local colour is worked into the story, not stuck on it. The writer shows immaturity at certain points where conclusions are expressed; and lies somewhat open to misunderstanding; experience and practice, if I may venture a suggestion not lying strictly within my line of duty as a judge, experience and practice and the cultivation of broad and tolerant sympathies will set that right. The faults of the story, besides those indicated above, are that we early see that one of two endings is obvious, and too soon detect which ending it must be; that the catastrophe is rather "mechanical"; that the writer lets slip opportunities that should have been used of "intensifying" and thus approaches rather too nearly the risk of being sketchy. But the story has the great virtue of artistic assertion in its*

subject. The writer is not thinking of the reader, of the GLEANER prize or of himself; he is thinking of "Lorita" and her fortunes. The gods have no higher gift than this absorption in the subject in hand to bestow on the Maker of Stories.

The allusion to Greek gods would have given Eddie great pleasure. In his writings, Eddie occasionally referenced classical literature, as in the title of his poem, *Lux Noctis,* and the character from Greek mythology in *Ariadne's Song,* the latter being a poem in which Eddie, as he does in *Lorita*, tries to think the thoughts of a woman suffering from rejection in love. In his first column of literary musings for the *Jamaica Times* he had recommended a translation of *Euripedes* by Gilbert Murray, a brilliant classicist and "a poet of high rank."[99] Euripides was known for representing mythical heroes as ordinary people in extraordinary circumstances and for focusing on the inner lives and motives of his characters in a way previously unknown.[100] Consciously or unconsciously following Euripides, Eddie had tried to understand Lorita's inner life.

MacDermot's high praise may be tempered today by the slightly Victorian melodramatic aspects of *Lorita* but the story's characterisations and key scenes are robust and memorable and it shows an acute awareness of colour and class. Eddie seats it firmly in the Jamaican countryside, most

[99] *Jamaica Times*, 6 June 1903, 14. Professor Gilbert Murray (1866-1957) would become Regius Professor of Greek at Oxford University and a founder of the Oxford Committee for Famine Relief (later Oxfam).

[100] *Euripides.* Wikipedia: https://en.wikipedia.org/wiki/Euripedes. (Accessed: 10 March 2018).

probably a landscape based on that around Glassonby.[101]

Until he won *The Gleaner* Christmas Story Competition in 1905 with *Lorita*, Eddie had written mainly under the pseudonym of E. Snod. From *Lorita* onwards, his works were published mainly under his real name, E. A. Dodd. Perhaps, having won a prize for a short story, he now felt confident in claiming his works.

The last four stories

After *Maroon Medicine* and *Lorita*, and following a gap of nearly four years, four more of Edward Austin Dodd's short stories were published: *Farder Matney's Pigs*, 1909; *Mr. "Simitt" Corn*, 1910, *The Obeah of 'Ole Shaw'*, 1911, all in the *Jamaica Times*, and *The Professor's John Crow* in *Pepperpot*, a compendium of stories, poems, and illustrations published by the *Jamaica Times* in 1915.

Farder Matney's Pigs

Although published in 1909, a story with the similar title of *Farder Matney's Two Pigs* had been submitted to *The Gleaner's Christmas Prize Story Competition* in December 1904. *Farder Matney's Two Pigs* did not win the competition but MacDermot, the judge, considered it to be amongst the seven best stories. Of these, MacDermot wrote that:

> *The competition here is good; the writers have clearly had some experience of their art, and as clearly love that art. It is noticeable that these stories, in conception and artistic force, representing* [the] *high water mark, so far as this*

---

[101] 'Newport', Eddie's place of writing at publication, was where Glassonby was located.

competition goes, are also those that show most care in the minutiae of composition.

MacDermot also thought that *Farder Matney's Two Pigs* was:

an excellent bit of dialect work. It shows careful and successful observation; but, regarded as a story, it is slight. The writing that connects the dialogue needs strengthening, and the dialogue itself is at times too trivial.[102]

Five years later, and no doubt improved upon, the *Jamaica Times* published it in its August Special issue.[103]

Farder Matney's Pigs is a comic tale in the vein of those in *Maroon Medicine* with a plausible cast of characters, particularly the tongue in cheek 'Cousin Will', gathered at the home of a Jamaican peasant on his supposed deathbed, dressed in their finest, singing, praying and scheming.

Not everyone enjoyed the story. Astley Clerk wrote a letter of complaint to the *Jamaica Times*. Clerk ran a successful music store in Kingston, The Cowen Music Rooms. He printed and published music works including his own and is credited with being the father of modern orchestral music in Jamaica.[104] Clerk felt that:

In the story the entire [teaching] *profession is held up, in the person of "George Smith," a teacher, to ridicule. Our teachers are not perfection, and none know it better than*

---

[102] *The Gleaner*, 17 December 1904, 4. On 10 November 1904, 10, E. Snod is listed as an entrant in the Story Competition. There can be no doubt that he was the author of *Farder Matney's Two Pigs*.

[103] *Jamaica Times*, 21 August 1909, 6-7.

[104] *The Gleaner*, 30 April 1961, 20.

they do, but I challenge Mr. Dodd to produce such a specimen as he gives us in "Geo. Smith," a man utterly incapable of fitting any other profession but that of a wharf-man … In fact if it were possible that Mr. Dodd is right and his specimen is to be found all who have the interests of this Island at heart should rise up and denounce the Mico College, the nursery of our teachers, as not doing its duty in passing men of the "Geo. Smith" type and sending them forth in their untrained and ignorant condition to teach the rising generation …[105]

MacDermot gave Clerk's letter the sub-title, "A Mistaken Interpretation", and, in a rejoinder printed below, he wrote that:

Mr. Clerk has in his enthusiasm mis-read Mr. Dodd's intention entirely. We took his little sketch not as suggesting that the "Teacher" introduced represented Jamaica Teachers generally, but merely as an odd and amusing figure in one individual case. The sketch is a bit of fiction and written, we are sure, without anything akin to malice, by a young Jamaican of marked literary talent. Mistakes such as that into which Mr. Clerk has fallen in misinterpreting the sketch of our contributor are, we suppose, inevitable, in a small community, but are one reason why we do not develop our Island talent. "George Smith" is no more to be taken as a type of Jamaica Schoolmaster… than Meredith's "Egoist" is to be taken as a representative of Baronets and a libel on them.

MacDermot's mention of the central character in George

---

[105] *Jamaica Times*, 28 August 1909, 17.

Meredith's 1879 novel, *The Egoist*, who is a self-absorbed man looking to marry, suggests that, in addition to George Smith in *Farder Matney's Pigs*, he might have also had in mind Mr. George Green, the teacher who pursues Miss Annabel in *The Courting of the Dudes*. It is possible that Clerk too may have been thinking about this character who has more affectations than Mr. Smith.

In the following issue of the paper, Eddie repeated MacDermot's assertion that no harm or malice was intended. His letter was sub-titled "MR. A. CLERK'S MISTAKE." Eddie assured that:

> *I had not the slightest intention of ridiculing the Elementary School Teachers either as a body or individually. I have too much esteem for them as an educating power, and their lot is one that I for one would like very much to see improved. There is no harm in a humorous drawing, and it is often a matter of individuality whether we laugh at a description or whether we are offended.*
>
> *It is without the slightest malice that the story was written, and I trust that most readers will take it in its own spirit. It was meant to be a humorous sketch from the kindly country parts.*[106]

The criticism does not appear to have harmed the reputation of *Farder Matney's Pigs*. Indeed, on 5 June 1912, a recitation from the story was given at a gathering of the James Hill Literary and Improvement Society, a community-based society in upper Clarendon that had been established in

---

[106] *Jamaica Times*, 4 September 1909, 11.

January 1912 with Claude McKay as Secretary and Mr. E. A. Haynes as President.[107]

This is an interesting event. McKay had only recently become known for his poems in dialect. *The Gleaner* had published a number of them to great acclaim in late 1911. McKay, then a policeman in Spanish Town, left the force and went home to Clarendon to work on his father's farm and write more poems for publication. He would spend about a year there working towards leaving Jamaica for the United States of America, never to return.

In the memoir that covered his life in Jamaica, *My Green Hills of Jamaica*, McKay did not mention the James Hill Literary Society (though he did write about the many tea socials that were put on in Clarendon in 1912 in his honour). A new figure-head in Jamaican literary society, McKay's community probably set up its society with him as secretary in order to encourage an interest in literature. Certainly, donations of books to the society's library came in from the Governor of Jamaica, the Director of Education, the Editor of the *Jamaica Times*, Jekyll, and others.

At the 5 June gathering, twenty-seven recitations – poems, short stories and non-fiction – and songs were performed, featuring the works of Claude McKay himself, Tom Redcam, and other writers of note at the time. One of the recitations was an extract from *Farder Matney's Pigs* read by Claude McKay's brother, Hubert. E. A. Haynes gave a speech suggesting that such an event could not have been held even two decades previously. Thomas MacDermot was present

---

[107] Establishment of such societies was also occurring around the Caribbean. Source: V. S. Naipaul, *A Writer's People* (2008), 4.

and wrote and published a complete account of the evening because it was:

> *so outstanding, so much in a line with the spirit and methods of the "Jamaica Times" and the policy it has pursued for years of trying to bring Jamaica Literary talent to the front.*[108]

The gathering has been referred to as "a unique cultural event" in the history of West Indian literary development.[109] MacDermot's effort and vision had helped bring to bear a literary climate in Jamaica that allowed such an event to occur. The inclusion of a work by Eddie gives him another small place in the history of Jamaican literature.

Mr. "Simitt" Corn (An echo of the drought, in south Manchester)

This story was published in the *Jamaica Times* in 1910, demonstrated a depth of feeling that was never to be fully developed in Eddie's writing. *Mr "Simitt" Corn* tells the story of a family driven to theft by drought and starvation. When he was not at school, Eddie would have spent his teenage years at Glassonby amongst the people of rural south Manchester. He would have well understood the impact of drought conditions on its poorest inhabitants. In *Mr. "Simitt" Corn* he outlines the background of a struggling family:

> [Sam's] *father had disappeared under the stress of the drought nine months back, and his mother had kept*

---

[108] *Jamaica Times*, 15 June 1912, 11.

[109] C. Cobham Sander, *The Creative Writer and West Indian Society* (St. Andrew's University, PhD thesis, 1981), 73.

herself and him and Lucy – his sister a little older than himself – by the little money they had got from pimento picking and a little occasional washing.

In a very short story the characters are as roundly developed as can be. These are real people who are suffering and in the grip of a dilemma. Unlike many brought up in the Victorian era, Eddie did not moralise; he was sympathetic and his final line had the initially unsympathetic shopkeeper, Mr Smith, appreciating "the greatness of the necessity that drove his fellows to such extremities".[110]

The Obeah of 'Ole Shaw'. A Jamaica Story

The Obeah of 'Ole Shaw' was the last story by Eddie to be published in the *Jamaica Times*, appearing in the Christmas Number 1911.[111] Set on a pimento and coffee pen, the tale examines Jamaican attitudes to the practice of obeah. The description of the property of 'Cave Valley' in *The Obeah of 'Ole Shaw'* perfectly represents the Dodd property of Glassonby in Manchester.[112] If one stands now at the old main entrance of the house, one can see Eddie's 'semicircle of sea stretched beyond the far plains.'

Clever young Will and his friend and accomplice, Thomas, play tricks on their work mate, the gullible 'Ole Shaw' who believes in the powers of obeah. At this time, the practice of obeah was the subject of serious debate in Jamaica. The

---

[110] *Jamaica Times*, 16 April 1910, 8.

[111] *Jamaica Times*, 16 December 1911, 25.

[112] The Glassonby property was sold to the United States Government during World War II. In the 1950s, the Dodd family home became the Curphey Home for Old Soldiers.

government was concerned that obeah men and women practitioners exploited credulous believers to make money and, in the process, created problems in communities. Eddie took the lighter approach and created a humorous story. 'Ole Shaw' is superstitious and Will and Thomas use his gullibility to amuse themselves and others but they all are sympathetic and likeable characters in their own ways.

The Professor's John Crow

This was to be Eddie's last published short story and it appeared in the *Jamaica Times* publication, *Pepperpot, A magazine depicting mainly the personal and lighter side of Jamaica life.* A substantial large format paperback printed in England, *Pepperpot* was an ambitious venture for the newspaper. *The All Jamaica Library* series had not been a financial success but *Pepperpot* was another effort by the *Jamaica Times* to publish works on "Jamaica and Jamaica Life in its many phases."[113] Thomas MacDermot must have overseen the project which was likely his idea but the editing work was undertaken by Reginald M. Murray and C. Thornley Stewart. The contents were by noted Jamaican writers of the day such as Murray himself, Frank Cundall, H. G. De Lisser, Claude McKay, E. Astley Smith and E. A. Dodd. The illustrations which must have been included with a view to boosting sales were by Thornley Stewart.

Thornley Stewart was an English artist who had lived in Jamaica for nine years, taught art at Jamaica College and was Secretary of the Jamaica Club, a meeting place for the upper echelons of Jamaican society on Hanover Street, Kingston. In

---

[113] *Jamaica Times*, 19 December 1914, 22.

October 1913, before he left the island to live in South Africa, he was awarded a silver Musgrave medal for his "encouragement of art in Jamaica". His nomination read:

> *Mr. Stewart has executed a number of portraits for public rooms, he has depicted Jamaica scenery, has illustrated a number of publications connected with Jamaica, has conducted successful Art Classes in connection with the Jamaica Institute, contributed effectively to the artistic side of the exhibits sent to the Toronto Exhibition from Jamaica, and has shown his versatility as well as his talent by excellent work as a cartoonist.*

The nominators went on to praise the artist's work that year which included "the painting of several large portraits of public workers, the illustration of volumes relating to Jamaica and the conducting of Art Classes."[114] Thornley Stewart had also made something of a name for himself by gently caricaturing many of the members of the Jamaica Club, portraits of whom he included in *Pepperpot*.

Reginald M. Murray, the other co-editor, no doubt handling the literary contents of the publication, was also a master at Jamaica College. A son of the Reverend Dr. William Clarke Murray, he was a cousin of Thomas MacDermot. He had sat the Cambridge University Local Examinations (with Eddie) in 1899, and won the Rhodes Scholarship in 1904. After taking his degree from Oxford, he returned to Jamaica and joined the staff at Jamaica College. He was to serve, with honour, in

---

[114] *The Gleaner*, 5 December 1913, 3. Publications connected with Jamaica that he provided illustrations for include *Jane: A Story of Jamaica* (1913), and *Twentieth Century Jamaica* (1916), both by H. G. De Lisser.

World War I, and become headmaster of, first, Wolmer's Boys' School, and then Jamaica College.

The Gleaner article of 21 October 1913 suggested that the publication of *Pepperpot* was imminent but it was to be over a year before the book was put on sale in Jamaica; this was in December 1914, though its date of imprint is actually 1915.

Eddie Dodd's contributions were his story and two line drawings (one of which may be the most pleasant illustration of a John Crow ever produced). The other drawing, dated 1913, illustrated a poem by Murray.

In *The Professor's John Crow,* the main character is a young engineer, Dick, who is living in Kingston next door to a retired headmaster and his daughter, Christine, who Dick is courting. There may be elements of the story that are autobiographical, such as sitting in a guinep tree with the object of his affections on a Sunday afternoon, with oranges from south Manchester.

Pepperpot sold 500 copies in two days.[115] However, despite its initial sales success and its publisher's satisfaction with the outcome, the book was not without controversy. In January 1915 the Mayor of Kingston, H. A. L. Simpson, addressed a gathering of Marcus Garvey's Universal Negro Improvement Association (U.N.I.A.)[116] Somewhat contrarily he denied that the people of Jamaica as a whole spoke as represented in the book but admitted that, if they did, then he was ashamed to hear them speaking in that way. He regretted the contributor Claude McKay "had not written after another fashion."

---

[115] *Jamaica Times*, 19 December 1914, 22.
[116] *The Gleaner*, 29 January 1915, 10.

Claude McKay had no qualms about using dialect in poems and, the year before, had written a well argued defence of doing so in a long letter to *The Gleaner*.[117] McKay felt that "the negro dialects of the West Indies and America" were a variety of English just as "English provincial dialects and… that of the lowlands of Scotland" were. He did not see "why writers should not express themselves in the dialect as they feel led [or] why Jamaicans should be ashamed of the dialect." McKay's arguments notwithstanding, Simpson appears to have been most concerned that the book would hold black Jamaicans up as curios and present a bad impression of them.

Perhaps *Pepperpot* did not appeal to a large Jamaican audience; perhaps it was not priced competitively; perhaps the print run was too high for its Jamaican market. Certainly, in 1922 it was being sold by The Times Store at less than half its original sale price.[118]

---

[117] *The Gleaner*, 7 June 1913, 4.
[118] *The Gleaner*, 4 March 1922, 4.

Fig. 5 Illustration for poem about a mongoose by Reginald M. Murray published in *Pepperpot*

Painting and drawing

During his early writing years, 1902-1906, Eddie also painted and drew. In December 1902, at the same time as entering the *Jamaica Times* Christmas poem competition, he entered a drawing, *From Slavery Time,* into the paper's Christmas Drawing competition. According to the judge, it won "without a minute's doubt".[119]

Following a similar event it had held in 1897, the Board of the Institute of Jamaica decided to hold a competition in Art and Crafts in February 1903 with a display of items at the Institute for a week in March. The categories covered a variety of drawing and painting subjects and techniques, and crafts.[120] The Institute, following the decisions of its judges,

---

[119] *Jamaica Times*, 20 December 1902, 10.

[120] The categories were: Fine Arts (Time Study), Free-hand Drawing

awarded some entries a certificate of merit or, in special cases, a medal. Eddie, no doubt encouraged by his winning the *Jamaica Times* competition, took part in the Drawing from the Antique (Time Study) Competition, and entered three works in the Black and White Competition, winning a certificate of merit for *The old gentleman of the Black Stock*.[121] (Norah Shaw, who painted the watercolour of Alligator Pond featured in this book, also submitted paintings to the Competition.[122])

In the Institute's 1906 competition, Eddie entered two items in the "drawing in water colour and in black and white" group. The *Jamaica Times* felt that he was "not at his best in figures" but that his prize winning *Pedro Bluff* was "light and airy, although sketchy, which is no defect."[123] The paper noted with pride that it had already published a copy of the *Pedro Bluff* drawing "from a sketch in black and white made by Mr. Dodd."[124]

Eddie entered three paintings into the 1910 competition: *On*

(Time Study), Drawing from the Antique (Time Study), Black and White, Flower piece in Oils, Landscape in Oils, Figure Subject in Oils, Flower-piece in Water Colour, Landscape in Water Colour, Figure Subject in Water Colour, Decorative Design, Photography, Typography, Cabinet Work, Artistic Pottery, Blacksmith's Work, Silversmith's Work, Art Needlework, Carved Cocoanuts, Wood Carving, Leather Work, and Jippi Jappa Hats.

[121] The painting's name may relate to the novel set in the southern United States, *The Old Gentleman of the Black Stock* by Thomas Nelson Page, published in 1901. *Stock*, in this instance, refers to an article of attire worn at the neck.

[122] *Jamaica Times,* 21 March 1903, 9.

[123] *Jamaica Times,* 10 March 1906, 16.

[124] This was in the *By Palm and Surf* series.

The Hill Tops, *Steamer at Wharf*, and *On The East Coast*. He won no prizes but the *Jamaica Times* noted that the "little fragment of mountain top… with its two wind-blown trees, is a charming morsel, carrying a touch of distinctiveness, to the impressionistic observer at any rate."[125]

Travelogue - *By Palm and Surf*

In late 1905 and early 1906, Eddie briefly returned to writing non-fiction. In 1904, a two- part feature entitled *Round the Island on the "Arno"*, describing a trip taken by a "Special Correspondent" on a Royal Mail Steam Packet Company's ship, had been published in the *Jamaica Times*. As the paper's "special representative", Eddie undertook a similar journey in the week before Christmas 1905. The *Jamaica Times* may have paid for the cost of Eddie's trip and, possibly, expenses, but there is a last minute quality to this undertaking with the trip taking place so near to Christmas and with only a month before the resulting articles were published. It may have been that Eddie, flush from winning *The Gleaner* Christmas Short Story competition that month with *Lorita,* suggested the trip to the paper, part paying for it with his prize money. (A cabin cost £3 for a round trip and Eddie had won £2 2s.) Whoever paid, the *Jamaica Times* was aiming to encourage interest in travel around Jamaica.

Ships of various companies travelled regularly between England and the West Indies and around the islands, carrying passengers, mail and goods, particularly bananas. They offered an alternative experience for tourists to that of a stay in a hotel or two with excursions around the island by land.

---

[125] *Jamaica Times,* 26 February 1910, 7.

They also took tourists to places that did not normally receive income from tourist dollars such as Savanna-la-Mar and Lucea. This addition to the tourist offering would have been something that MacDermot and Durie would most likely have wanted to encourage. The introductions to Eddie's articles stated the intentions of the *Jamaica Times* and suggested its pride in what Jamaica could offer:

> *The following account was written by a special representative of the JAMAICA TIMES, MR. E. A. DODD, who recently went on a coastal trip in the R.M.S.P.'s well appointed s.s.* Arno. *The pictures illustrating the series are prepared from sketches made by our representative … The articles should do something to bring home both to Jamaicans and to visitors from abroad the healthy pleasure to be had in a trip on the Arno along our beautiful coasts and that at a very low cost.*[126]

Earlier in the year, the *S.S. Arno* had been thoroughly overhauled and refitted and cabin passengers had on board the luxury, for the time, of electric lights and fans.[127] The ship also carried a number of deck passengers at much lower rates and some of these captured Eddie's attention. In his first article, Eddie described boarding the ship at Alligator Pond and the trip to Kingston where he stopped off for a week. The next four articles cover his voyage from Kingston, initially westwards, round the island and his excursions ashore at Black River, Savanna-la-Mar, Dry Harbour [Discovery Bay], St. Ann's Bay, Ocho Rios, Port Maria and Port Morant. He described views of the coastal scenery, loading and

---

[126] *Jamaica Times*, 3 February 1906, 2.
[127] *The Gleaner*, 13 February 1905, 11.

unloading, incidents on board and other aspects of the voyage, and his adventures onshore, exploring, swimming, sketching and looking up old friends. However, it is the faithfully recorded conversations in dialect that are the vignettes that transform Eddie's otherwise satisfactory account into something more vivid.

Eddie's reading on board almost certainly included the 1899 book, *Negro Nobodies* by Jamaican Noel de Montagnac, and the recently published *Negro humour* by J Graham Cruickshank from Demerara, British Guiana. Eddie was clearly drawn to tales from the West Indies that featured dialect. It is conceivable that, as well as amusing himself, he was studying them in order to see how he could improve on the genre.

With the voyage taking place in the last full week before Christmas, indeed arriving back in Kingston on Christmas Eve, and the deadline for text and drawings in a month's time, Eddie did not have much time to "cut and file" his English prose.

The five articles in the series, *By Palm and Surf*, were published in January and February 1906, not far into the start of the high tourist season in Jamaica.[128] They were accompanied by twelve sketches Eddie had made during the journey and a banner header drawn by John de Pool, the *Jamaica Times* special artist who had "studied art in Europe and America" and whose services were also employed by the Times Engraving Company.[129] As the *Jamaica Times* rarely, if ever, in this period provided such a banner for its pieces, this suggests the editor's likely regard for Eddie's work.

---

[128] *Jamaica Times*, 27 January, 3, 10, 17 and 24 February 1906.

[129] *Jamaica Times*, 12 January 1907, 5.

5 THE SIGNIFICANCE OF E. A. DODD'S STORIES

After his death, Eddie's writings were, largely, forgotten. Nevertheless, because he followed his own advice and wrote about what he knew – Jamaican life, its customs, country and people – his work is worth reading today.

His short stories give an impression of an early twentieth-century rural Jamaica where life is unhurried and relaxed. It is the same Jamaica that appears in Claude McKay's novel, *Banana Bottom*, and in his memoir, *My Green Hills of Jamaica*. It is not the Jamaica of the 1930s where pressures of population growth and economic difficulties were to bring about political crises.

Most of Eddie's work is light in nature but in Jamaica comedy is a vital element of life.[130] Eddie described Jamaican people with humour, compassion and sensitivity. He clearly liked and admired his fellow Jamaicans who, throughout his rural upbringing and railway career, he would have heard talking to and entertaining one another. His characters, despite their brief appearances, are well-rounded and real. Reading their words, they them seem alive today.

Edward Austin Dodd and Thomas MacDermot shared a common cause in their appreciation of Jamaican stories and people and in their desire to promote Jamaican literature. *Maroon Medicine*, which followed *Becka's Buckra Baby*, firmly

---

[130] That most skilled Jamaican writer of the twentieth century, Louise Bennett-Coverley, conveyed subjects and themes of the utmost seriousness and depth through her comic and witty poems, pantomimes, and radio dialogues. The more recent *Roving with Lalah* series of articles in *The Gleaner* also describes encounters with Jamaicans in a humorous style. See also: *Roving with Lalah: Slices of Everyday Jamaican Life* (2012) by Robert Lalah.

established a Jamaican short story genre where the prose is in standard English and speech is in Jamaican dialect.

The Collected Works of Edward Austin Dodd

6 SHORT STORIES

MAROON MEDICINE

[from "Maroon Medicine", 1905]

It was just one of the cottages that you see scattered all over Jamaica; possessing four walls made of plaster and lathes, and a thatched roof – the whole enclosing two rooms, dignified by the names of bed-room and hall. From one corner stretched a small barbecue, which again at one corner fed a small "Kick-um-buck" tank, covered over with rough logs to prevent people falling in. All around, for the space of about half an acre, grew in picturesque medley, coffee bushes, yams, breadfruit trees, orange trees, the products of the lower mountains in the Parish of Manchester. A couple of fowls scratched around the house and a hungry-looking pig messed about his little railed in pen.

It had rained in the night, but the morning had broken exceeding fresh and fair, warm yet cool, with a bright beauty that I cannot believe could have been surpassed anywhere. It may be that the pig felt something of this, or it may be that he knew that his morning meal was nearly ready, but undoubtedly he felt happy and showed it in little unmusical squeals. His master sat at the edge of the barbecue, chopping up into a box with his cutlass, steadily and with attention, a few small canes. Having finished chopping all except one choice bit which he reserved for his own consumption, he rose and went to the pen, where he put the box before the pig. He then proceeded to chew his own piece of cane, with a certain amount of intelligent repose on his face.

This face of his was long and of a neutral brown, with

the bony chin going in sharply up to the neck. The man had a wide and mobile mouth, with a quaint twitch at one side, two small twinkling eyes and a bald and sloping forehead under his hat of plaited thatch.

It was a perfect morning in the end of November, yet to judge from the slight frown which crept up and marred the repose of Mr. Watson's face, one could not think the latter was in sympathy with nature's peace. The reason was simple, Mr. Watson had very little ready money; and Christmas was coming, and he felt aggrieved with himself and his wits, which were not in the habit of failing him. His thoughts ran in this groove:

"An a what me got fe Chris'mas bar dis little maugre pig? Me cawfee no sell well, and me premento don bear, a what me got? Me we have to do sompin?"

His musing was suddenly interrupted by the approach of a neighbour who was walking through to his ground, and who stopped to salute him.

"Hi, mornin' Miser Watson!"

"Mornin', Coz! How you do?"

"So, so, sah, a not too well an' a not too bad. You a feed you pig, sah."

Mr. Watson turned carelessly and twitched the few scraggy hairs that formed his whiskers, with a gesture peculiar to him.

"Yes, sah, me a feed him, but a wha de use? I buy him back dis tree weeks from Miser White at James Hall, and I gie'm yam peelin', cocoa head, banana an' all sort o' ting, an look pon him now, h'no ah piece fatter than when I buy him. Well (with emphasis) as you might seh, a doan pay much fe him, but it tan like a not goin get no more fe him."

"Hi, but a wha do de pig den?" said the neighbour sympathetically. "Him really ought fe fat. Aldo some of dem, a so dey tan. I remember dis man Joe Crawford got a pig; well when he buy him, h' not too fat so h'n get plenty o feedin', cane, cocoa head an' I don know what; an' him feed that pig fe true, but you believe me sah, dat pig was no fatter at de end of tree monts dan when he got him fus' time. Mus a same way wid dis."

Mr. Watson looked with a philosophical calm at the pig.

"Well, it may be. Ah same way wid some man; you wi see some o' dem eat, eat, an eat and yet dem never get fat, dey tin all de time."

"You speak true, sah, a same way wi some men."

After a pause the neighbour hitched his bankra better on his shoulder and said:

"Yes, sah, ah jus' a walk trew to me groun' go look somepin for me wife."

"You welcome, you welcome," said Mr. Watson hospitably, "a no hear you wife sick? A fe true?"

"Yes sah. It true! night before las' she tek in wid a single pain in de stomach. De pain hol' her dat way. Well she go to bed, an' ah tek dis bush dem call "Piobba" and a bwoil it down and mek some tea, gie 'er but it doan any good, den ah mek some oder tea out o'dis other bush, "Vervain," an' gie 'er dat, but dat also doan do any good; and all dis time de pain dat bad. Well yesterday about sun hot, Mrs. Weekly advise me try some soda and nut oil mix wid a little water and I do so, and since then she feel a little better and could walk bout de yard in the evenin'. Yes sah she really sick but she not too bad dis morning."

During this speech Mr. Watson showed his sympathy in a few well chosen sounds and affirmatives which cannot be reproduced by any combination of letters.

"Ah glad fe hear she better. Some of dese teas is really wonaful. To be sure some doctors good. I woan seh dey not, but mos' time you go to dem, you jus' wase you money. Dis bush or dat is all I want."

"You right, Miser Watson, you quite right," agreed the other heartily. "Some doctors no wut a grass louse, aldo dis Doctor Pratt him really good." Then moving on, "Well ah gone, Miser Watson."

"Yes, sah." Mr. Watson sent him on his journey with a wave of his hand and then resumed the reflective chewing of his cane. I may remark here that the man's ground was five miles away, but there is nothing strange in this; for the Jamaica Peasant will travel up to ten or twelve miles to get some fresh piece of land to till and work as a ground. Every two or three years he throws up one piece and takes another fresh bit.

After his friend's departure Mr. Watson's face took on an even more reflective look; and for half an hour he lolled in deepest thought; then straightening with a brightened face, he walked into his house, and emerged with his jacket on, having been without it before.

His face now was the calm inscrutable and cunning face of Mr. George Watson of Every Garden. This was the name of his place, but how it had arisen, and what was its origin, Mr. Watson himself did not know.

He left the house and yard now in charge of a little ragged girl, his daughter, and took one of those paths which fed the main road like tributaries of a river. Coming out on this, he walked for about three miles, when he came into a village consisting of two or three rival shops which sold various assorted articles, from very weak rum to a drawing book, and a couple of professional houses of shoemakers and blacksmith. At one of the former he bought a sixpence worth of soda, and between the three, two dozen pint bottles, saying in sort of excuse that Mrs. Smith (who made bread) had asked him to buy the former for her, and as regards the latter, he was speculating in bottles, and was going to sell to a man from Kingston. He also gave out that he was going up to the Mile Gully Mountains to invest in ginger.

Having bought what he wanted, and having refreshed his mind with a little light conversation, he left and went home where he was busy all day mixing in the privacy of his half-tumbled down kitchen, some vile-looking stuff.

It was perhaps between four and five next morning when Mr. Watson started for the Mile Gully Mountains "to invest in Ginger", driving his donkey, yclept Alice, before him. The hampers contained the two dozen bottles he had bought the day before, a dozen on either side, empty no longer – also some little provision for his journey – a gill bammy[131], a little pork already boiled, some yams and some oranges. His house he had locked up, but the pig and the cultivation around he had left in the charge of his neighbour and daughter. This latter by the way being driven from under the paternal roof, had taken up her abode for the time being with her aunt (?). She was not Mr. Watson's only child, having three brothers and a sister alive. These, however, having come to the conclusion that their father was not perfect in his ideas regarding obedience in his children, had severally run away to other yards, a common enough practice in Jamaica. Needless to say, Mr. Watson did not go after them. His was a philosophical soul and he in no way regretted not having to feed three hungry children. He would not have received them back; and his children knew it.

By the time the sun had risen and another perfect day had begun, Mr. Watson had passed Mandeville and was nearing Williamsfield. On reaching the latter place, he stopped near the Railway Station under the shade of an overhanging roof of a front house, and sitting down proceeded to assuage his hunger with half the bammy, half the pork, and half the oranges. The yam was destined to be roasted and eaten higher up when he had come to the end of his journey.

After half an hour's rest, Mr. Watson rose, stretched himself, and started again with a touch and a word to Alice.

From here onwards his road led higher and higher,

---

[131] A "gill bammy" was a bammy that cost three quarters of a penny.

and at about mid-day he entered the district he was bound for. At one or two houses near the road, he enquired his way to the yard of Mr. Hezekiah Brooks. This Brooks had once travelled his way and had partaken of Mr. Watson's hospitality, the latter putting him up for a couple of days. He undoubtedly would now in his turn be glad to put up his former host. After about half an hour's walk, Mr. Watson came to the Brooks yard and found the gentleman of the house at home, who welcomed him and expressed his delight at seeing him again. Mr. Brooks was a small brown man, a carpenter by trade, of not much force of character, yet kindly and good-natured.

"Ah really glad fe see you, Miser Watson. Don mention it, sah. Jus' tie you donkey to dat tree and step dis way. Me no ha much as regards house and place to sleep ina, but weh me hav, you welcome to."

Over some roasted yam and boiled saltfish the little man took upon himself to find out why Mr. Watson had come up that way.

"Excuse me, sah, and I doan mean nutten by it, but ah curious to know whey you travel dis way fur. You mus' be going buy and speculate?"

Mr. Watson resting easily against the side of the kitchen twitched his whisker:

"Well you guess right enough, Miser Brooks, I am goin' fe speculate, Ah did notice dat our way, well dem doan grow ginger or nutten to speak of, an' de backra ladies dem, dey always a want ginger. So I tink if I buy some up dis way an' tek it down, a might a mek a little pon me bargin." Mr.

Brooks looked at him.

"Yes, sah, you might a really mek sompting pon it. Me neber tink o' dat, or me might ah try it before. You mus' be going carry it, de ginger ina bottle, me notice you got plenty o' bottle."

Mr. Watson ate his saltfish and remarked indifferently:

"Oh de bottle only got a little Maroon Medicine in dem. It such a good thing for sickness dat I tink dat as a coming up here wey dey doan know it and colds is plenty ah could ah sell a little here or dere."

Mr. Brooks got so interested that he stopped eating.

"Weh you call it, sah, Maroon Medicine? Me no hear 'bout it before. A wah it good for?"

Mr. Watson took a bite out of his roast yam.

"Well, down our side, dey use it for all sort o' sickness, but specially for boile, and stomach ache and cold wid fever. A see plenty o' people cure wid it."

"Me would a really like fe try it;" said Mr. Brooks. "Me daughter, Susan yah, often trouble wid stomach ache. How you sell it sah?"

"Well, as it mek out a somptin' dear enough, me sell it at shilling a bottle, but as you is a fren' a would a gie it to you for sixpence."

"But it's really good, Miser Watson?" asked Mr. Brooks.

"Well it is not for me to praise me own ting, aldo in dis case it really not mine, for I didn't mek it, a Maroon mek it for me, but of all de medicine and fever bush I know, none cure you so quick as dis. But of course if you doan want it, well den doan buy it."

Mr. Brooks hastened to assure his friend that he meant nothing by his remark.

"A only want fe know, Miser Watson, and me tink me wi tek a bottle, sah."

Mr. Watson sold a bottle to Mr. Brooks and the latter promptly made Susan take a small dose, which undoubtedly had a certain medicinal effect by night.

Towards five o'clock in the afternoon the two men took their way to the popular rum shop in the neighbourhood, Mr. Watson wisely leaving all medicine behind, trusting to Mr. Brooks to advertise him, The little man was of a loquacious turn of mind and that evening certainly lived up to Mr. Watson's trust. Over a glass of weak rum and water he told in graphic terms how he had given Susan one dose not two hours ago, and already

"It hab a wonaful affeck!"

Mr. Watson when questioned about it gave polite but modest answers, only asserting that he had got an old Maroon to make it up for him, the latter assuring him that they used it a lot among his people and he, Mr. Watson, had indeed found it good. Towards half-past seven Mr. Brooks and his guest returned home where they found Susan emitting groans at intervals and rather sick. Mr. Watson comforted her and her father by assuring them that she would feel much better by morning and that the medicine always made one feel sick at first.

Next morning Susan was much better and radiant at having taken such a "wonaful" medicine. She had no pain and said she had a great appetite. Her father was delighted and Mr. Watson felt cheerful himself, having had up to now certain doubts about the after effects of his medicine. He sold six bottles that day, taking over ginger and home-made ropes in part payment, where the buyer did not have sufficient cash. They went out again to the shop in the evening, and Mr. Watson found himself being rapidly advertised. He was asked several times how it was made and what of, but he refused to tell saying that he had promised the Maroon not to. Various guesses were made at its composition which produced a desire in every person to taste it, and by the end of a week Mr. Watson had sold every bottle, and he found himself regretting he had not brought more with him. Most of the people who had taken it felt much better for having done so. Making the most of his job, he loaded his donkey once more and started for home, giving out that he was going for more medicine which he would sell more cheaply this time. He reached home after another half day's travelling and found after selling his ginger etc., he had realized one pound five shillings on his adventure. Not being satisfied he made more medicine, and after Christmas sold to an appreciative market on the Mile Gully Mountains.

In conclusion I should say that soon after Mr. Watson had left the Mile Gully district the second time, some slanderous and evil reports got abroad about him, and the numerous buyers of his "Maroon Medicine" were heard to say that "dey wish dey could a catch dat ----- man agen, dey would a gie him medicine fe true!"

PACCY RUM

[from "Maroon Medicine", 1905]

It was about 3 o'clock in the afternoon – the hour when the sun seems brightest and hottest in the tropics. Along the heavy grey sand of the beach were ranged a number of black canoes, some high up from the sea, – these had come in from early morning – others which had just been beached still on the wet shore. On the horizon, the sails of a few late fishing boats could just be seen appearing on their way back from their fish pots. They would reach White Bay, as the bend in the shore was called, in about an hour's time. The gunnels of the boats which had last come in were thickly lined with women and girls, buying fish from the fishermen, and making a loud clamour over the business. The atmosphere about was heavy with the strong raw smell of fish, in all states, live fish, dead fish, fish boiling, fish roasting, and fish being cleaned. The sea was dazzling with a thousand lights, glittering on the moving wave tops, especially in the west and more directly under the sun; out in the South-east and far away under the low lying and purple hills, it was a rich blue, and nearer, but in the same direction, a tender green. From the bay and following the shore was a long line of cocoanut palms bending over towards the water and looking top-heavy, with their heavy masses of boughs. Separated from these and so near the canoes which were selling fish, that the rush of the foam almost reached the roots, were a couple of palms affording at their curved bases seats which were generally occupied. Under the shade of one of these palms a middle sized man, with a long bony face and small eyes and large "weh-fe-do" hat, was bargaining with a woman for two small mullet. The woman had bought a string of fish – of which the mullet formed a part, for sixpence a few hours ago, and was now trying to get the man to pay "quatty" or penny-half-penny for about the eighth part.

"Oh, but Miser Watson, you can see dem wut quatty! dem wut more if it come to dat, but sake ah you, you can tek dem fe quatty!"

Mr. Watson slowly stroked his whiskers and wrinkled up his eyes to shut out the glare which was on the sea.

"Well, Miss Jane, you seh dem wut quatty, and I tink dem wut gill, and if dats what you goin ask all de time fe dem, ah wi hav to guh look elsewhere."[132]

The woman looked at the fish and at Mr. Watson's face undecidedly, then bending over her tray:

"Mek ah tie up me fish den, you want too much fe you money, sah!"

Mr. Watson shouldered his "bankra" and turned to go with such final decision in his movement that it made the woman say hurriedly:– "Alright, Miser Watson, see you fish yah!" Mr. Watson turned and putting down his "bankra," took the fish calmly and gave the woman her gill, which she received with a deep sigh, that would have deceived no one:

"Lard but it cheap! Dem tek advantage of a poor ooman!"

Putting up the fish carefully, Mr. Watson shouldered

---

[132] A quatty was one quarter of a sixpence; a gill was three quarters of a sixpence.

his bankra again and turned away with a "well ah gone, Miss Jane," to which the woman accorded a gracious "yes sah!" in a tone of voice whose kindliness one did not expect from her former bargaining.

Quitting the canoes and people Mr. Watson walked a little way up the beach, then turned at right angles on his left, up a path which after a minute, brought him out on the main road. For about a mile he walked along inland when, coming round a bend in the road, he entered a small village. Though small, it was, however, of some importance as one could easily see, for it had a Market, a Post Office and a Police Station. Through the gate of the Station Yard he turned in and walked up to a Constable who was sitting in shirt sleeves on the piazza of the house. The station with its yard, like all other Police Stations in the Island, was scrupulously clean and well-kept; and there was the usual air of neatness and respectability about the whole that spoke well for the discipline of "the Force."

"You come back quick!" said the constable to Mr. Watson as the latter approached him.

"Yes sah, me nuh top no time down ah de beach. Ah jus buy me two little fish dem an come back fe me bundle and donkey to start fe de mountin."

"Well see you bundle deh!" said the constable pointing to a corner in the piazza where a shallow open box lay filled to overflowing with coloured cloths, handkerchiefs, etc., and bound round with a thatch rope. Mr. Watson entered the piazza and putting down the bankra, untied the rope and proceeded to pack the upper clothes more neatly.

Having arranged them, he put a piece of oil skin over all and strapped the whole again.

"What you going do wid dem stuff?" asked the constable with a smile, as Mr. Watson finished his repacking. Mr. Watson turned and looked thoughtfully at the constable:

"Well, sah, ah doan know what ah goin do wid dem rightly. Ah may keep dem, ah may sell dem, well den of course you wun know bout dat." Here the constable laughed and said "You speak true, I wun know bout dat."

"Because," proceeded Mr. Watson gravely, "ah no got no license, but to tell you de troot, corporal, ah doan know rightly what ah goin do wid dem."

"Well ah doan tink I wi know meself, bar you tell me!" answered the Constable who was not a Corporal by the way, but just an ordinary policeman.

"Oh I wi tell you alright, when ah come down agen!" answered Mr. Watson as he lifted his box out to where a donkey was tied under a lignum vitae tree. He strapped, or rather roped the box on the donkey's back, which also bore the burden of two hampers, then came back for his bankra.

"Ah no hear that some man or other did da sell rum widout a license up your way?" said the constable, as Mr. Watson gathered up his guiding rope and prepared to start.

Mr. Watson rubbed the side of his face slowly, and answered as if in deep thought. "Now you remin' me corporal; ah did hear bout it, not up my way to be sure, but down ah Mary Town. But I neber hab anyting to do wid such wickedness, so ah carn tell you fe true as I neber come into contack wid dem. Well, ah goin, corporal!" he added as the Constable did not say anything more.

"Yes sah" answered the Policeman with a grunt.

Giving the donkey a fillip with the rope, Mr. Watson started and was soon out of sight of the village and on the road leading up to the hills where his home lay. Shortly after he had left the station yard, the Constable with whom he had been talking went into an inner room of the station house and remarked to the real Corporal who was sitting at a desk writing.

"Him no got any rum this time, Corporal! I did really tink me'd ah catch him." The Corporal turned round; "I did tink so meself. Did you look in his box properly?" The Constable nodded "Well, Corporal, ah raise up all de clort dem and ah see no sign of it. But you tink a man would ah leave hie box wid rum slap ina de station piazza? Him no fool!"

"Fac! It is a fac!" answered the Corporal musingly. "Him mus' ah hear dat we are on the look out and tek warning; nex' time ah goin search him properly doh."

"You right, Corporal!" answered the other, "Him wi sure got some dat time. But, Lard him cunning sah."

Meanwhile, Mr. Watson, not entirely unconscious that he was being talked about, was wending his way slowly up the steep beginning of a long hill. By sunset he had got over the more arduous and bigger part of his journey, and by about eight or nine o'clock he entered his own yard. He unloaded the donkey and gave her over to the charge of his daughter, a girl of about fifteen years, who, taking her, gave her drink and tied her out in a grassy patch. Mr. Watson put up everything carefully, taking a special care over six large quart bottles which he had found wrapped up in some clothes at the bottom of the box. The very boldness of his action in leaving his box with six bottles of rum at the station had brought him safely through the hands of the police. Then he went to bed after a hot dinner of breadkind and salt fish.

During the earlier part of the next day Mr. Watson took it easy, resting doubtless after the weary journey of yesterday. Towards the latter part of the afternoon, however, he went out to the village of Beersheba which was near his place, and stayed there two or three hours. He seemed to have gone there with some purpose, for next day he had plenty of visitors, who first examined his cloth and handkerchiefs, then bought according to their liking. He also managed to exchange his six quart bottles for silver coin at a price double what he paid for them. By evening he had got rid of all his cloth and stuffs and was plainly satisfied with the results of his undertaking. "Dem Constable ah watch me fe true, Lorita", said he to his daughter in the privacy of their kitchen as he sat smoking his dirty-looking clay pipe.

"Dem search you box no sah?" answered Lorita with eager interest stopping for a minute in her work of peeling some sweet potatoes.

"Yes chile! Dem raise up all de clort dem at de side wen ah down at de Bay. Dem neber really look clean tru' it, because dem neber dream dat ah would ah leave rum slap ina de station, but dem look ina dey." Lorita laughed out loud with the noisy intonation peculiar to her race, and said:

"Lard but you fool dem sah!" Mr. Watson even permitted a feeble sort of grin to pass over his face which showed he was very much pleased with himself, for he never went so far as to laugh and seldom to smile. "Wen you going down agen sah?" asked Lorita after a pause.

"Tree week from yesterday to come," answered her father. "But ah wi have to tink out some odder way of hiding de rum, or dem wi sure catch me nex time."

"You no can tek pass tru' somebody yard or some oder road, no mek dem see you?" asked Lorita, plumping the potatoes into the big iron black pot.

"No me chile, dem ah look out fe me and dem would ah certain fin' me, aldo ah might ah risk it, and try mek ah fool dem same time. Ah really might ah try it," said Mr. Watson, gazing thoughtfully with half-closed eyes out at his donkey which was browsing on some Spanish Needle near the coffee bushes. "But," he added, "ah not trying it agen, bar dis one time. Ah doan seh ah doan mek some money out ah it, but it too risky, it too risky. You can fool dem Constarb to-day, an' you can fool dem to-marra, but dem wi catch you some time. You carn fool dem all de time. So ah only going try dis once more." Lorita gazed with some admiration at her father after this truly profound and philosophic speech and grunted in affirmative approval.

"You right, sah, you really right. Me always ah tink dem going ketch you."

Mr. Watson continued to himself, "Yes, sah, me really

mus fool dem dis time, or else not, me wi know Panish Town inside, and learn how fe eat carnmeal. Dem planth'n roas' yet, Lorita?"

*   *   *   *

About three weeks later Mr. Watson again took his way down to the plains, and about four o'clock in the afternoon having accomplished a little transaction of his own at a Sugar Estate, was wending his way back home. His donkey was heavily laden with hampers containing stuff of a weighty nature, and in the outskirts of the village near White Bay, he stopped to adjust the hampers and body ropes more easily. He then continued at a brisker rate through the village, past the shops and market, till he approached the gate of the Police Station Yard. Here he slowed down and, in an indifferent and leisurely manner, walked past the gate. He had not gone two yards past however, when he was stopped by a shout from the same Constable that had taken charge of his baggage before. "Miser Wason!" Mr. Watson stopped and turned.

"Miser Watson! a word with you sah! Bring you donkey in too!"

Mister Watson led the donkey back and turned within the station yard where he was met by the Constable and the Corporal.

"Marning, Miser Watson!"

"Marnin' Carporal! marning Sargent!"

The Corporal then addressed him.

"Sarry fe stop you, Mister Watson but some people ah seh some tings bout you, dat you ah sell rum widout license, so as it is my jurisdiction and duty, ah wi have to search your hamper, jus' fe prove dem is arlright."

Mr. Watson at this speech, looked at the Corporal, as if he did not understand him, then, stroking his hand on the side of his face, he said slowly:

"Dat I ah sell rum widout a license?" Then after a pause, he led the donkey forward and said gloomily as if overcome by the wickedness of people, "You can search him."

The two proceeded to search the hampers while Mr. Watson stood silently by with a look of cold impassive dignity on his face. The Constables quickly took off the "cruckcuss bag", or bag of sackcloth that covered the contents of the hampers. They then saw that each hamper contained two kerosene tins, covered over at the tops with a piece of cloth tied down tightly. They removed one of these pieces of cloth and saw to their disgust nothing but thick "wet sugar" which filled the pan almost to the brim. They tried the other three and found them just the same, full of wet sugar. The Corporal tried to hide his disappointment and disgust under a cloak of outward good humour.

"People will tell lie Miser Watson," said he, "an ah really lose me drink dis time. Pan sugar is really better to trade in dan rum doh, an ah sorry fe hab to trouble you."

Mr. Watson waited in silence till they had tied back the cloth and put in the bags, then he began: -

"Well, Sargent, you hab you duty, and you tink it right, maybe dat you should ah stop an hones' man ina him way, to go hol' him donkey and search him like any common tief slap ina de public. But I doan tink it right." Mr. Watson's voice rose higher, "I doan tink it right. Seh help me, if ah doan tink you treat me like any common dirty tief dat dem haul go ah Spanish Town. If dat---"

"Go on you way and doan mek a noise in de yard," said the Corporal, angry at his failure to find rum and the hypocritical defence of Mr. Watson. "Go out de yard."

"Ah goin, ah goin!" said Mr. Watson moving out. "You tink ah would ah stay yah in dis place, weh dem mek me out a criminal; an hones man got no place ina dis yard."

With this parting shot Mr. Watson and his donkey took their way out and went again on their journey home. Long after dusk he reached his yard, where he found Lorita anxiously looking out for him.

"As ah no see you come by sunset, an it ah get late" said she, "me seh dem mus' ah really catch you dis time, sah. Me really anxious fe you." She helped him unload the donkey and move the hampers inside the kitchen, then gave the beast a little water and tied her out for the night. Returning to the kitchen she filled her father's plate with breadkind, roasted and boiled, yams, cocoas and plantain, the whole flavoured with pork and country pepper.

Mr. Watson made a hearty dinner and during the meal gave an account of his meeting with the Constables, and how he fooled them, to his daughter, who listened with much interest.

"An den, as ah come to de station yard gate, ah tek time walk slower fe mek dem tink ah warn go pass widout dem see me, as if ah no care. De Corporal and de Sargen' tan up inside an watch me – dem really not any Corporal and Sargent but so I call dem – an' as ah could ah get bout one yard pas' de gate, de Corporal cry out loud:

"Miser Watson, Miser Watson, ah warn see you. Bring in you donkey, come too ina de yard."

Well, when ah hear dat ah turn roun' as if suprise, and lead de donkey ina de yard."

"You no feel frighten, sah?" asked Lorita as her father paused to put a big piece of "nager" yam in his mouth. Mr. Watson masticated for a few seconds before answering:

"Well, ah doan seh ah doan feel kine o' funny when ah hear me name call sharp, but of course ah doan mek dem see it, but jus' lead me donkey in quiet, an tell dem marnin'. Well den, dem tek off de bag quick fe true, an as dem see de kerosene tin, dem eye jump, and dem whip off de clort quick as anyting."

Mr. Watson paused again to take in some more food and give power to the climax of his tale.

"An what dem seh when dem see de sugar?" asked Lorita eagerly.

"Dem neber seh scarcely a ting," answered her father, "dem so disappoint. Dem could ah only smile an' look like dem torm fool bud. Dey neber would ah guess in dis worl' dat rum could ah ina wet sugar ina paccy. But you tink de paccy doan fit de kerosene sweet!"

"Weh you get dem sah?" asked Lorita, "down ah White Bay?"

"No me chile," answered Mr. Watson, "ah get dem higher up de beach, at a place dem call it, Lef River Hole, where dem grow like Premento grow yah almos'. Ah fill dem firs' wid de rum and stop up de hole tight, den put dem in de kerosene tin an' fill up de tin wid de pan sugar. Dem could ah neber fine it out."

Mr. Watson by this time had come to the end of his dinner, and he handed over the plate to Lorita, who washed it and put it up in its place on a shelf with a couple of pans and cracked mugs. Her father who was tired and sleepy then went to bed, Lorita following his example, and they were both soon sleeping, if not the sleep of the just, yet the sleep of undisturbed consciences.

THE RED COCK

[from "Maroon Medicine", 1905]

Fig. 6 Advertisement for *Maroon Medicine*, 09 September 1905

CHAPTER I.

Wherever two or more roads meet in Jamaica, there is, as is doubtless true for other parts of the world, generally to be found one or more shops. Sometimes the situation is important enough to demand first one shop, then a village, then a town, then perhaps a large city according to the development of the country. Jamaica has not yet got many towns however, and the one shop usually becomes two or three with a couple of other houses around, and is then called a village. In this state it generally remains, and probably will remain for many more years. Beersheba belonged to this class but it had to show, as a sign of some advancement, a Post Office; and the Tax Collector came at his times to receive taxes there. It lay in the southern part of the Parish of Manchester and had roads leading from it to Mandeville and Vere and St. Elizabeth; from which it will be seen that it had a good position.

About four or five years ago it was celebrating with much noise and fervour the 1st of August. Very few, if any, of those who celebrated remembered why it was a public holiday, or brought that forward in their enthusiasm; still they were recognizing it with games and sports. About a hundred yards from the shop, in a field which formed a sort of suburban part of the village, the annual Cricket Match between Beersheba and Smithfield was going on, and was being played with much spirit. The pitch consisted of a long naked piece of land; all its grass having been rubbed off by continual running upon, and it was very red and very dirty. As the players went to and fro they gradually partook of its redness in their clothes and socks (for most played in their socks alone). It took a lot however to tint the original colours of some of the socks, these being very brilliant in hue – purple, and yellow, and red. These facts did not detract from the enjoyment of the game, and the pitch was certainly more level with the grass off. The spectators, other than the men of the team now batting, were chiefly women and girls selling bread and cakes and ginger beer. The absence of the men was due in a measure to the fact that there was a game cock fight just about to begin outside the saddler's shop, and there thirty or forty men were collected round two who had a cock each in their hands. Game cock fighting happened now to be very much in vogue, and like all other transitory amusements had a good deal of enthusiasm behind it. The present fight was between Mr. Joe Robinson's "High Licker" and Mr. James Bolton's "Harkaway," and the stakes were £2 a side. These stakes were formed from twenty shares of two shillings each, ten of which had been taken by an owner of one cock, the rest being divided among ten other shareholders. Thus either cock had eleven enthusiastic backers, not counting the interested spectators who indulged in independent bets and shouting. The referees were two shopkeepers, and men of standing, as one could easily perceive from their dress and high dignity of bearing. Among those nearest the cocks, with a long and grave face, was a shareholder in the company which favoured Mr. Robinson. He took great interest in the proceedings, but did not grow loudly excited as the others did. His name was Mr. William Watson of Every Garden, this being the name of his place. Suddenly the chief shopkeeper raised his hand, –

"Let them fly," said he and the owners raising their birds flung them at one another. Mr. Robinson's bird was smaller than the other, but looked more game to experienced eyes. Either fowl had had its spurs cut off and a sharp long piece of steel substituted, clumsily, in their place to produce a more deadly battle. The cocks now began to spar in earnest and various opinions were passed and good humoured remarks:–

"Hi! Miser Robinson! You fowl good, you know. Him little but h'n 'trong."

"Come on now, I wi' bet you five poun' dat de red cock beat; yes me son, five poun'!"

"Five poun', Lard me Massa, ah since when Charlie get five poun. H'n mus' ah tief it from old Fader Dennis!"

"Choh no man!" said another, "He mus' a going married to dat yaller giurl from Queentown. You no hear she got money."

"Shut you mout, you impudent chap you!"

"Hi! Miser Watson, ah bet you a sixpence 'gainst you raw-bone jackass dat de yaller cock beat!"

There was some laughter at this, but Mr. Watson disdained to answer. He only scratched his side whisker.

"Hi, de yellow cock ah gie de oder all him looking for! Miser Robinson, I gie you quatty fer you cock!"

"Quatty and gill!" yelled another. Here a shout went up:– "Fus blood, for Miser Bolton Harkaway!"

"Hah, what ah tell you, I know de yaller cock would ah win!"

"Cho, man, him doan win yet. You wi soon see him favour Johncrow when h'n going dead."

The odds now were in Bolton's favor and the red cock seemed indeed going to lose, when suddenly he began to attack with fury and jumping up high, came down with a cruel slash across the head of Harkaway, blinding him in one eye. A great shout went up:–

"De red cock beat! De red cock beat!"

"Him doan beat!"

"Him do beat; you no see him wun get up!"

"H'm no beat, ah tell you!"

"Ah wha ah tell you! Han up me sixpence!"

"Han up which sixpence? ah owe you any sixpence!"

"Doan mek ah get angry yah, today! Did you not gie de sixpence you bet wit me to George Bent to hol', and den tek it weh when you see ah going win?"

"Oh man de bet off!"

"De bet off what! you is a d---m wutless scoundrel!"

"Ah who you ah call all de wutless scoundrel? Jus' call me so agen!"

"You *is* a scoundrel!"

The one struck the other and a scuffle ensued. They came apart and took on an awful appearance of most deadly hatred. One feared for their lives.

"Now you jus' strike me agen!"

"Strike you wha! You strike me fus?"

"Jus' strike me! You jus' hit me!"

"Well you jus' hit me fus', and I wi' show you what you want!"

It ended in each requesting the other to hit him, but as the other refused to do such a rude and unchristian act, the quarrel evaporated gradually. During this the yellow cock had fallen, and refused to get up though urged by his owner to do so. The referees then adjudged the victory to Mr. Robinson's High Licker. As soon as the red cock had beaten the other to the ground, it might have been observed that his eleven backers had shoved in round the stakes holder, and when victory was declared, hastily took their money from him and also their rival company's. Plenty of vigorous language was being shouted on all sides as the losers tried to get out of their bets and the winners urged their rights. By one of those powerful unwritten laws which hold all the world over, Mr. Robinson had to stand drinks for the defeated company and everybody adjourned to the most popular of the rum shops which, by the way, belonged to one of the referees. Here for two or three hours, plenty of shouting, argument in very curious English, and some quarrelling which ended in words for the most part, went on. The negro does not as a rule need much rum to make him tipsy, for a very little affects him. He seldom however gets really very drunk or intoxicated to that extent that he cannot go home without help. This is true for the country parts, where the lack of ready money, perhaps has something to do with the soberness of the people. Nearly every shop outside the towns in Jamaica sells rum and other intoxicants, but this does not mean that there is an excess of drinking among individual parties, but rather that nearly everybody takes a drink now and then. After an half hour's conviviality Mr. Robinson, who was rather cautious as regards all his money affairs, took his cock and started for home accompanied by his wife and Mr. Watson whose home also lay in the same direction.

"You going home soon," said Mr. Watson to Mr. Robinson, "You not going join in de spoart at de shop?"

"No sah, no port for me, ah win me money fair, ah wah ah going spen it for? ah hab one drink, dat's all, ah want more?" "Tell me," he added half angrily and half drunkenly to Mr. Watson, "Tell me sah, you tink a man should ha' spen' and wase h'm money pon de ting dem call rum and get drunk like a beas. Dem is a fool."

"You speak true sah," said Mr. Watson soothingly, "Dem is a fool. But sah, when ah see you fowl beat, ah really glad. Him is de bes' bird bout."

"Him good, him really good," agreed Mr. Robinson, whose anger passed away at once, excessive amiability taking its place. "Did you see how h'm rise up and slash de oder cross de head? me heart leap till ah tink it going pop, when ah see h'm gie dat blow."

Mr. Watson eyed the bird with grave admiration, "Wunderful, sah, wunderful! An' how much," with a differential air that flattered Mr. Robinson, "would you be askin' for a cock like dat sah?"

Mr. Robinson looked at him as if he did not understand. "An' how much would ah ask fe him?" he repeated. "But him not fe sale. You tink ah would ah sell dis fowl; ah woulden sell him, not even if ah ah dead fe hungry, an me belly swell out like dem little maugre pig. Ah bring up dis cock from de berry egg shell, and ah watch him and see him grow to dis size and den ah going sell him?"

"No sah, you don understan me," said Mr. Watson, hastening to pacify the other; "ah don mean to ask you how much you would ah sell him for, but what, jis out of curiousness, you tink him wut? Ah no hear dis man Thomas

Simit seh him would ah gie ten shillin' fe him?"

"Ah know, ah know," said Mr. Robinson, "h'm offer me dat already, h'n na sell."

"Me hab a little money from me tobacco and premento," said Mr. Watson musingly, "if ah could get a real good bud like dat, ah would ah buy him. Doh ah mus' seh dem is a risky ting to keep. Dem may beat and den agen dey may lose an' you no know when dem going sick."

"My fowl na going sick!" said Mr. Robinson as if in protest to some remark against his cock.

From these casual remarks, Mr. Watson gradually led up to the direct question of asking Mr. Robinson to sell him his fowl, and he was in full persuasion when they came to the meeting of the two paths which led from the public road to their respective homes. Finding Mr. Robinson obdurate and quite opposed to any business, Mr. Watson scratched his right whisker philosophically and said good bye.

"Well as you wun do any business Miser Robinson and ah doan seh you wrong, I mus go me way. Evenin' sah! Evening! Miss Ann!", this to Mrs. Robinson who had been walking, as a wife should, about ten yards behind her husband.

"I wish you a good evenin' sah!"

It was dusk when, after a couple of minutes walk from where he had separated from the other two, Mr. Watson entered his own yard. His daughter, a ragged girl of about twelve, had preceded him, and had stirred up the fire in the rotten shaky looking kitchen to greater vigour by the addition of some wood. The walls of the kitchen were of plaster white-washed outside, but lacking this dressing inside. The inside however, to make up for the coating of white-wash had taken to itself several coatings of soot and was very black and dirty especially near the fire corners. From the rafters of the thatched roof hung bundles of tobacco leaves which were being cured in an atmosphere of peculiar smell, born of smoke and other odours. It is easy to recognise this smell when, on a pleasant summer evening, a man will pass on the road smoking his "donkey rope." The seat of honour, a polished block of wood, stood near the fire, and around were various odds and ends, old pans, cocoa heads, a donkey's pack saddle, etc. This room was Mr. Watson's study, dining hall, pantry and kitchen. When Mr. Watson entered and took his accustomed seat, the girl was stirring a pot of red peas soup, and a little boy of grave long face, inherited doubtless from his father, was sitting in one corner eagerly awaiting his dinner.

"You feed de pig yet Josiah?" asked Mr. Watson of this little boy.

"Yes sah, me feed him dun dis long time."

"Ah want you go wid me to de groun' tomorrow to help me carry some potatoh slip," said Mr. Watson, "ah doan wan mek de season pass."

"Me have fe go up to Cedar Valley tomorrer go bruk premento sah!" said Josiah in his shrill young voice.

"Hi fe true," said Mr. Watson. "I nuh fuhget. You tell Miser Tom dat you wun tek fipence a day?"

"Yes sah, but him seh sah, dat if ah doan wan de fipence, ah fe stay way sah."

Mr. Watson gave a grunt and was silent. The soup was now ready and the girl poured it into three receptacles, a blue soup plate with a yellow border, which as being the only soup plate belonged to Mr. Watson naturally, a cracked mug which the girl kept for herself, and a tin pannikin which the boy eagerly accepted. They had pewter spoons however of the same pattern, design and size. After finishing his soup and some roasted potatoes the boy departed to his bed, which was a sort of bench in the hall of the house proper. On his leaving the kitchen, his father began a conversation with his daughter:–

"Lorita, ah offer Miser Robinson eleven shilling for his cock dis evenin' an he wun tek it."

Lorita who was a thin featured and sharp looking girl looked at her father then laughed, "Him mus a fool."

Mr. Watson fingered the few hairs that formed his right whisker: "You speak true, Lorita h'n is a fool. When a man see eleven shillin' in h'n han' h'n should a sell. You no know when time mongoose goin' tek you fowl or h'n may dead or h'n even walk way."

Mr. Watson then lowered his voice and proceeded to whisper cautiously, "Stop you laughing Lorita and listen to me. Ah been tell all o' dem dis evenin' dat ah goin to me Uncle a Santa Cruz tomorrow, so dey won know. Ah going start ina morning soon an' you mus come down Thursday night (it was now Monday) to de Bay cross roads whey I wi meet you. You certain you know wha fe do? eh?" Lorita nodded.

"Ah know fe certain sah, ah could ah walk bout dat yard ina blackes' night."

"Well ah speak to you enuf to mek you unerstan an' you ought to do it right. But ah wi tell you over agen."

Mr. Watson kept on whispering loudly and earnestly to Lorita for about half an hour, then both went to bed in their palatial family house.

CHAPTER II.

On Thursday morning about seven o'clock, Mr. Robinson having rubbed the sleepiness out of his eyes by a vigorous application of water to his face, — this was generally as far as the bath went with him — strolled leisurely round to the back of his house to look at his fowl. To his astonishment he found the door of the coop open and its occupant absent; thinking however that his wife had loosed the cock to have a run, he went back to quarrel with her, for he had given her no permission to do any such thing. He learnt from her, however that she was innocent of the charge, neither was any one of his children guilty. His feeling then became one of terror and anxiety, and he and his household looked long and eagerly for the cock. The news spread quickly among the neighbouring yards, that Mr. Robinson's Red Cock was gone, and by about ten o'clock it become apparent that the fowl had been stolen.

Mr. Robinson now was frantic and his language would have been interesting to the thief if he had been around.

"Ah wish to Gawd Awmighty dat ah could ah hol de man dat tief me fowl. Me Gawd, ah would ah kill him! Ah would ah tear h'n inside out. But whah sort o' man dem hab bout yah dat h'n should ah come slap ina me yard ah night and tek out me fowl. De dam blarsted tief!"

Having given up all hope that his fowl had strayed, Mr. Robinson put on his coat and set out for the nearest Police Station, which was about four miles away He took some time to walk the distance, as he stopped several times to relate the news to sympathizing friends, and give candidly his opinion of the thief's character.

On arriving at the station, he told his story to the Corporal in charge, and gave a minute description of the fowl, leaving out, however, the fact that it was a game cock. The reason for the latter reticence being that game cock fighting was not allowed by the law. The Corporal told him that he would have the description of the cock sent around through the *Police Gazette*, but said that as Mr. Robinson did not suspect any one in particular, there was nothing much more to be done.

"You certain that you got no suspicion 'gainst any man at all?" he asked.

"No sah, me no got any suspicion," answerered Mr. Robinson gloomily. "Dem is all a tief." "But if ah hav' fe spen ebery penny ah got, ah wi punish him," he added vindictively. He then tried at the neighbouring shop to find consolation in a couple of glasses of weak rum and water, but the rum only helped to inflame his passions and he returned home very angry and sullen. His way, when coming to his yard, took him very near Mr. Watson's home, and in passing he might have noticed Lorita fast asleep under a banana tree in some coffee bush. He might have noticed too that she looked very tired, but these little things went unseen to his clouded intellect and be certainly would not, even if he *had* noticed her weariness, dreamt of associating it with the absence of his fowl.

About this very time or a little earlier, Mr. Watson and his "raw-bone jackass," Alice, entered the yard of his uncle "Old Father Matney," after a walk from the bottom of the Manchester Hills. Father Matney's yard was some miles south-east of the village of Santa Cruz, and Mr. Watson and his donkey were rather tired, for the road leading up from the Savannas into the Santa Cruz Mountains is a monotonous and wearying climb, over stiff and numerous little hills. When Mr. Watson entered the yard of his uncle (he was supposed by some to be his father), he found the old gentleman asleep under a mango tree with a bible open in his hands. Father Matney had been rather a wild fellow in his younger days, so to make up for lost time, had taken enthusiastically to religion in his old age. At present his inclinations tended toward Seventh Day Adventism, but he had not become a regular convert and his mind was still open to any taking ideas that might come along. He welcomed his nephew cordially and gave him breakfast which his daughter, a good looking woman of a sort of yellow colour, dished up for them. The name of this woman was Eliza Matney, and she had that peculiar yellow colour of skin which is seen chiefly in the people of the Savannas and hot plains of the Southern and South-western parts of the Island.

"You bring anything fe me Willyam?" said Mr. Matney after the donkey had been unloaded and tied out and they were eating their breakfast. Mr. Watson finished swallowing some boiled potato before answering,

"Well sah ah doan bring nutten much, but knowing dat provision is scace down dis way, ah bring you a couple o' yampi an' cocoh."

"Tenk you me son, tenk you," said the old man, "The blessing of de Lord fall pon you, for you tink bout de ole man an you len to de Lord."

Mr. Watson chewed his yam modestly:–

"Well sah, me doan go to Church ofen, an de collection man dem, doan ofen see me money, an ah swear and all de res' o' it, but ah do tink pon me relations sometime."

"Well Willyam," replied the old man who liked yampie, "so far you bad enuf, but when you gie to me, de poor ole man, you lenin' to de Lord, you lenin to de Lord, an de Lord will repay you, for h'n seh so and h'n hab to."

"Ah notice you hab a cock wid you," changing the subject abruptly. "What you goin do wid it?"

"Ah buy it cheap from a man up ah Plowden," answered William, "ah did hav' de money an it so cheap dat ah buy it for a shillin!"

"Shillin?" said Mr. Matney, "It cheap, an a game cock too?"

"You right sah," said Mr. Watson, "ah game cock, an because ah game cock ah buy it. I bring him fe try a fight wid de cock bout yah."

"Cock fightn Willyam?'" said Mr. Matney, "you going in fe dat, you wi lose money, an' besides it's sinful. Aldo you is a young man an you mus hab you way. When you is my age, well den you wi tink more about gettin you soul ready for de great day. But me no hear dat dem doan allow it by law, dat dem can punish you."

"Dem doan allow it fe true!" agreed Mr. Watson, "But if dem doan know, how can dey punish you?"

"Well de station is far enuf away,'" said Mr. Matney, "an ah doan suppose dey wi catch you. But dese tings is sinful, Willyam! Bery sinful."

Mr. Watson did not think it worth while to take up the question of its sinfulness, and went on eating without making a reply. However, Mr. Matney, finding his nephew unwilling to discuss cock fighting from a religious point of view, limited himself to the financial and social sides of the sport. For an old man who was supposed to be wrapped up in the pursuit of religion, he showed a surprisingly keen knowledge of his neighbours' affairs, what sort of cocks they had, and the latest fights that had come off.

"It really curious, Willyam," remarked Mr. Matney, "dat as you comin' to see me you should a buy a game cock, an you no know dat dem ah fight cock up yah. It really curious."

"You speak true sah" said Mr. Watson gravely, "it really curious."

"All tings is in de han of de Lord" said Mr. Matney without intending any irreverence.

Mr. Watson learnt from Matney and Eliza that a certain Philip Brown living two miles away, had a cock that had beaten nearly every other cock in the district. It would be easy to get up a fight between the two cocks, for Brown was keen on the sport and had won plenty of money on his. Mr. Matney seemed doubtful about the advisability of fighting such a good cock without trying theirs first, but Mr. Watson assured him that his cock was quite capable of beating any cock around, and he was going to Mr. Brown's in the morning to arrange the combat.

Next morning Mr. Watson found Mr. Brown quite willing to have the fight, and it was arranged that a duel, with a bet of ten shillings a side, should come off at Ole Matney's yard between the two cocks.

At noon then of the next day, Mr. Brown with his fowl and small party of backers went to Mr. Matney's yard where they found awaiting them, Mr. Watson with his fowl and his backers. After a few preliminaries such as placing the stakes in the hands of some worthy man and appointing two judges, a ring was formed round Mr. Watson and Mr. Brown and the fight began. During the fight a man who had but lately come from Manchester was struck with the resemblance between Mr. Watson's cock and a fowl, which he said belonged to one Mr. Robinson who lived near Beersheba. "Ah neber see two fowl favour so;" said he, "Aldo said ah do see a difference. But dem do favour fe true."

"You right, Marse John," said Mr. Watson heartily, "Ah know Miser Robinson fowl eben more dan ah know dis, an ah neber see such a likeness. Same so de oder one red!"

"De berry same!" said Marse John, "only fe you cock little smaller!"

"Ah tink so meself" agreed Mr. Watson, "Him little smaller."

The fight took place with less noise than at Beersheba, but it was longer and more game. After about ten minutes severe sparring however, Mr. Watson's red cock first wounded and then completely defeated the other and his owner was richer by ten shillings.

After the shouting had stopped and some hostile arguments had passed off, Mr. Watson and Mr. Matney brought out some glasses, some rum and some water; and everybody had a drink in the red cock's honour. Mr. Matney, who had a strong belief in the idea that all things little or great that profited him, were the work of Providence, and that anything that was unfortunate was the work of Satan, was especially joyful and even took a drop of rum in excess of good fellowship. Mr. Brown and his party finally took their departure about an hour later, taking with them however, an open challenge to anybody in the district, who having a cock might like to fight.

As the result of this challenge, no less than four fights came off during the next two or three weeks, of which Mr. Watson's cock won three, and his Master – we will not say owner – gained £2 in all. It is to be feared that Mr. Matney's soul did not benefit by Mr. Watson's stay, and he had, for several lapses in sinfulness, to make up by many outward signs of remorse and much bible reading.

At the end of the third week however, Mr. Watson sent Eliza Matney's little boy to Lorita at Every Garden with some tobacco and a message, and two days after the boy had come back, he departed himself from his uncle's yard. He went away at an exceedingly early hour of the morning, near midnight in fact, and by some strange coincidence met Lorita at the foot of the Manchester hills on his way to Alligator Pond at about two o'clock in the morning. Lorita did not stop to talk, however, but started off back home at a very quick walk, while her father went on in a leisurely manner to the bay. Two days later he returned home and found all the neighbourhood excited over the curious way in which Mr. Robinson's red cock had come back to his coop after a disappearance of three weeks about. Mr. Robinson himself did not know what to make of it, and meeting Mr. Watson on the day of the latter's return, expressed his opinions:– "Well Miser Watson, such a ting sah! Fus' ah lose him an ah sure somebody tief him, and den when ah ah look after to fin' de tief, de fowl come back. De only ting sah, is dat eider some man tief it an' put it back because h'm frighten o' me, or dat it some o' dem blarsted obeahman tricks."

Mr. Watson stroked his whisker thoughtfully:– "Well den ah doan tink it's obeahman Miser Robinson, from what I understand; but rader dat it's some tief, who mus' ah tek it weh and as you seh, h'm so frighten dat it put h'n back. But dayse wickedness sah!"

THE COURTING OF THE DUDES

[from "Maroon Medicine", 1905]

CHAPTER I.

"Heh, heh, heh eh … ! Doan bodder me son! But coo Thomas nuh! But Lar! Dayse trouzez and de gaiters – jus ah boasy! You ah go courting, nuh Thomas?"

Thomas for answer made a quick grab at the small barefooted boy who thus impertinently addressed him; failing to hold him however as the latter had been expecting the grab and easily escaped. Thomas in the glory of Sunday clothes did not think it worth while to go after him so merely remarked in tones that were not very vindictive:–

"Alright Hezekiah, you jus' wait yah till ah come back from chutch! Ah gie you arl you looking for. You too bloomin' farce."

Hezekiah at this merely laughed a shrill young laugh and followed his brother out of the yard, – at a respectable distance however. Thomas's get-up was certainly one to evoke attention if not admiration in all other people. His shoes, beginning from the bottom were of the fashionable colour brown, and of a peculiar and stylish cut, being a sort of cross between a shoe and boot. They were not high, nor yet low, buttoned by two rows of four buttons each, yet also laced with broad brown laces. Just above the shoes, sufficiently high to give a glimpse of a purple sock, came the end of a remarkably fine pair of light coloured gaiters, tailor made of corduroy and fastened with large buttons. The light colour of the gaiters was in fine contrast to a pair of dark brown trousers, which appeared also to advantage against the brilliant hues of a sash which looked like silk, but which, it was to be feared, was only coloured cotton or cretonne. Above this encincture shone out in dazzling splendour a full expanse of white shirt, with silver studs all complete. The coat which bounded this snowy bosom, was of a bright blue shade with a large handkerchief hanging half-way out of the breast-pocket, hiding the end of a silver chain which passed from the first button hole and had several large and ornate charms hanging to it. His hat, a new stylish felt, bought only a week ago, rested lightly on the "brush top" of his head, which was held a little stiffly by a high collar, girt at its base by a red and green necktie. The tie was kept well in place by a necktie clip of ornate and chased design, bought of a Syrian peddlar. As jewelry, other than the charms of his watch-chain, Thomas had two silver rings on a little finger, one of which had its value enhanced by a large red stone cut like a seal. He carried an orange stick, or rather a cane, nicely varnished in his hand, and had as a finishing touch to a masterly and most effective get-up, a gorgeous ginger lily in his button hole. Thomas was undoubtedly *the* Dude of the district.

They, – for Hezekiah was also going to church and was also dressed in Sunday clothes, which unlike those of his brother consisted simply of a blue suit and cap, – proceeded along in silence following a path which led over a stone wall into the pasture of a property or pen, through this pasture then over another stone wall and into the public road. Thomas did not walk too quickly for the day was warm, and the heat might take a bit of the polish off his appearance. To prevent any risk however to his collar, he stuffed his handkerchief round his neck between the skin and collar during his journey through the pasture; coming out on the highway he removed the handkerchief back again into its former elegant position.

As he and Hezekiah came into the road the first person they met was Mr. George Green, a teacher, riding on a young and rather small horse. Teachers in Jamaica generally ride, and it is strange how one can easily single one of that class from a crowd without any foreknowledge that he be a teacher. There is a mixed air of respectability, some bumptiousness, some self-assurance, some timidity, some importance, that always gives them away. Mr. Green in his way, was also a bit of a dude, not so flashy or bright as Thomas, but as befitted an older man and a teacher, more given to dress that showed solidity and dignity in its foundations. On this occasion he sported a pair of leather leggings, black and shiny, a rather dark suit with its coat cut long, and a collar, the lowness of which was due to the thickness and shortness of the neck it encircled.

Mr. Green greeted them with an affable and slightly condescending smile:– "Good morning Thomas! morning Hezekiah!"

Thomas answered with a rather absent-minded "Mornin' sah!" for the sight of Mr. Green riding so stylishly and with such dignity to church had set him thinking about his chances in love against such a rival, for be it known, Thomas and the teacher were rivals for the hand of fair (meaning comely) Miss Annabel Gibson who could not make up her mind which to choose. Thomas had the advantage of seeing her far more often than Mr. Green, whose duties kept him busy, and although up to now she had seemed gracious to him, still she had not refused altogether the advances of the other, and the position and comfortable salary of the teacher often obtruded themselves on his mind and made him gloomy. For some little way along the road his mind was thus melancholy, but the cheerful salutations of acquaintances that he met bound for church, added to the brightness of the morning, gradually dispelled his gloom, and by the time the church had come in sight round a corner of the road, he was feeling quite good humoured. Besides, was he not going to have the privilege of walking home with Miss Annabel after church!

Mr. Green had gone on ahead presenting, by the help of a martingale as well as a curb and snaffle bit on the mouth of the horse, a stylish and spirited appearance.

When Thomas had walked through the gates of the church yard, past the church and up to the school house, he found Mr. Green talking to Miss Annabel and her mother Mrs. Gibson under a mango tree.

He was neither surprised nor dismayed however, for he felt that off his horse the teacher was not such a terrible foe, so he took off his hat gracefully and shook hands rather bashfully with Mrs. Gibson and Miss Annabel. Mrs. Gibson, who was dressed in a much starched print gown that stuck out around in stiff folds, accorded him a kindly, "How you do dis morning Thomas?" and Miss Annabel, who looked charming in a white dress trimmed with bright blue ribbons and girt at the waist with a belt, also of a blue ribbon, gave him a gracious "Mornin Thomas." Thomas felt that he had not got himself up for nothing.

As they had a few minutes to wait before the service would begin, they remained under the mango tree for the time chatting; or rather the teacher and Mrs. Gibson chatted, the younger two being self-conscious were silent enough.

"How is Mr. Gibson?" asked Mr. Green of Miss Gibson. "I doun see him in attendant anywhere." "No sah," answered Mrs. Gibson, "H'n not yah to-day; H'n not feeling too well dis morning; H'n nuh really what you would ah call sick, but jus' enuf to no mek him warn go a church."

"Perhaps doh," said the teacher looking about him, "the mornin' is so bright and warm, it might have do him good – Been efficacious."

"You speak true sah. It might ha really do him good," said Mrs. Gibson, "but h'n jus 'tan so but h'n doan feel incline."

"Well however, de family well represent," said Mr. Green gallantly, "an Miss Ann look so agreeable dis mornin'."

At this Mrs. Gibson said, "Hi Misar Green!" while Miss Ann turned her head away with a bashful giggle. Thomas did not appreciate the teacher's compliments but he made the best of it and grinned too.

The bell-ringing had now come to a stop so they all went into the church to take their seats, being joined at the door by Annabel's sister, Susan, who had been talking to some other people.

The Gibsons occupied a pew on the gallery upstairs, and Thomas took a seat in a pew not far off, but the teacher being a man of some consequence in the church had a seat downstairs in the body of the church.

The service went on as most services do in the country parts, with plenty of late arrivals coming in every now and then. The young men and young women in Jamaica of the lower class do not consider that boots are worth anything in style or appearance unless they (the boots) creak exceedingly loudly, so the reason of any young man coming in late is probably to show off his clothes and boots.

After service, Thomas and the two Miss Gibsons stayed in for Sunday School which of course Mr. Green attended, being indeed one of the class instructors. When the Sunday School had finished, Thomas and the two girls started for the Gibsons' residence, Mr. Green having first bidden farewell, squeezing Miss Annabel's hand tenderly on the act.

The three walked along the road back, the way Thomas came, for the girls' house lay in somewhat the same direction as Thomas, save that they would not go through the pasture.

The order and manner in which Thomas and the girls walked home was rather peculiar and not, to appearances and foreign eyes, the most sociable. Instead of the three walking side by side, they walked separately; Thomas keeping to one side of the road and the two girls to the other. The girls did most of the talking and giggling, though Thomas every now and then would break in with a facetious remark from across the road. They reached Mr. Gibson's place after what seemed a short walk to Thomas, and had a cheerful lunch of bread and sugar and water. Then Thomas went home feeling somewhat satisfied, but not entirely so.

CHAPTER II.

On the Wednesday after the Sunday Miss Annabel received two letters from the Post Office at Beersheba. She did not open them at once, because it so happened that though she was a well brought up girl, she was unable to read, and she wanted the addresses read out in all their importance first. Her sister Susan who also could not read was as much excited over them as herself, and the two giggled and guessed to their hearts' content. It is not impossible that both knew intuitively whom the epistles came from.

However, during the middle of the day they went over to the neighbouring yard of a certain Mr. Richard Timson, a kind hearted man, who having had a much better education in his youth than those of his rank was looked upon as the scholar of the district, and usually called upon to transact any literary business, such as letter-reading and letter writing of his neighbours. This Mr. Timson was rather a character in his way. As a boy and young man he went to the Mico in Kingston, and after that took up teaching on his own account. Not finding this to pay, however, he went to Colon and was also in the stoker line on board a ship for a short time. After a time, when only about thirty years of age, he got tired of moving about and returned to his home in the country and took up life again as a labourer and settler. He had a higher sense of honour than possessed by his fellows, and was kind-hearted and cute, though a bit of a rogue.

Mr. Timson had just finished his breakfast when the girls entered the yard, and was sitting with his back against his kitchen wall picking his teeth. "Mornin' Miser Timsin!" said the girls approaching. "Mornin' Miss Ann! Mornin' Miss Sue!" answered Mr. Timson pleasantly. "You come to see me?" "Yes sah!" answered Ann shyly, "Me come fe ask if you could ah read two letter fe me; dat ah get dis mornin'."

"Ah love letter?" asked Mr. Timsin looking up at them with a smile.

"Me no know sah!" answered Ann with a giggle. "How me fe know what kind o' letter dey is, if ah doun read dem."

"Where de letter?" asked Mr. Timson.

Ann produced them and gave them to him. Mr. Timson looked at them with interest. The addresses were in widely different styles of hand writing. One was written in a quick ornate manner, with large flowing capitals and plenty of flourishes; the other in a small manner with very little flourish. Mr. Timson read out both addresses carefully and slowly, though they were just the same:–

Miss Annabel Gibson

Happy Home,

Beersheba P.O.

Finishing the reading he rose; "Come chile, mek we go in the Hall. Love letter not fe read out a doors!" So saying he entered the Hall which with the bedroom made the House, followed by the girls. He took a seat in a stiff home-made mahogany chair and gave the girls a bench. Having put on his spectacles as a necessary part of the insignia of a scholar, Mr.

Timson opened the letter with the large ornate writing and began to read out slowly and carefully:–

"Beersheba School,

12 Aug. 1900 ---

Dear Annabel,

As I take up my pen to write you these lines, I feel inmesurably the limitation of the body, which cannot express what my heart feels for you. Do you love me? If so tell me quickly that my mind might rest – for I cannot sleep night or day – my mind is so fix on you. I would like to see you face to face that I might have then throw off the burden if I know you love me. Will you be at the Picnic at White Hall on Saturday? I will be there and hope to see your dear face and hear that you love me. I hope your father is recovered, and that you are well. You do not know how my whole mind and physic."

When Mr. Timson got to "physic" he stopped. "Physic! Physic!" he said thoughtfully, "what you mean? De man ah talk bout him Physic as if h'n ah tek medicine. You know what him mean Miss Ann?" Miss Ann twisted her handkerchief:– "Me no know sah."

Mr. Timson read it out again, "Physic! But stop!" It suddenly dawned on him, "Oh fe true, him mean physique, which means de body or constitution. You understand?" The girls nodded and he went on. "You do not know how my whole mind and physique fix on you, and my spirit is crying for you. *Do, do* come to me. I am coming to a close. Give my best regards to your parents, and please accept 100 kisses

133

from me, who is and always will be

Your loving and dear well wisher,

George Green."

"Well, Miss Ann" said Mr. Timson, looking at the letter as he finished, "Dat ah proper love letter! You going tek him?"

Miss Ann held out her hand for the letter:–

"H'n too foolish!" said she. "Tenk you sah. Gimme dat and read de oder."

Mr. Timson handed her the letter and, opening the other, unfolded the sheet and read as follows:–

"Lang Syne.

13 Aug., 1900.

Dear Ann,

When I was with you on Sunday, I meant to have tell you of my love for you, but when it come to the front all courage leave me. How weak we are in the presence of that whom we love! How can I make you know how much I love you? From when we was young and going to school I love you up to now. Sometime I think you love me a little, and then again my heart ready to sink. Tell me darling, do you love me? The ring is round and has no end, so is my love for you. Are you going to the Picnic at White Bay on Saturday? I shall be there (D.V.), and shall get my answer from your dear mouth. I cannot stay here if you don't love me, so please don't send me away. Give my regards to your mother and father and receive my love and kisses.

Your loving one,

Thos. Bonito."

Mr. Timson read out the name of the writer with a kind of pompous flourish, then looked at the letter again as if admiring the writing. "Well, ah doan know how you feel, Miss Ann," he said, after a little pause, "but I like dis letter better than the other. But it not my business. Which one you going tek?" he asked with a smile.

"Tek wha?" answered Miss Ann loudly, "me going tek any o' dem? Dem too fool. Weh me got fe do wid love letter and such ting. Gimme de letter sah!" Hereupon Miss Ann began to laugh and giggle, which showed she was rather pleased to receive two love letters.

"Well it not my business;" said Mr. Timson giving her the letter, "but to tell you the truth and I carn deny it, if I was you I would ah tek Thomas, ah know him from a chile and you know him too an' h'n would ah suit you bes. But of course you wi please youself and ih not my business."

"Me like Thomas better meself;" said Susan. "De teacher too high an' mighty fe me."

Ann was silent and gave no opinion, simply tugged at her dress and laughed. After a little she rose, "Come Susan!" said she, "mek me goh." Turning to Mr. Timson, "me tenk you sah fe read de letter. It really kind o' you."

"Oh, no trouble at all," said Mr. Timson, "me always like fe read love letter, an of course I'm not the wan to say anything 'bout them."

"Tenk you sah," said Ann gratefully moving with Susan out through the door.

As they went into the yard Mr. Timson shouted after them, "Miss Ann, you going to the Picnic?"

"Me na know sah," answered back Miss Ann. "Dem too foolish."

Mr. Timson smiled at the answer as he sat in his chair, and it was really a charming smile so full of kindliness, good humour and wisdom.

"Ah well," he muttered to himself with a sigh as he rose.

"Dem is young. I hope she wi tek Thomas." But he added, "Ah really write that letter of Thomas well. De teacher nowhere with me."

Saturday the day of the Picnic broke cloudless and exceeding fair, and for its appointed time kept bright and warm with the bright warmness that the black man loves. Everybody was in good spirits and Mr. Honeyman who was giving the picnic seemed to be going to get a lot of money. The picnic entrance fee for grownups 6d., for children 3d., had been advertised all around and promised to be a success, for by three o'clock, an hour after it opened, plenty of people were on the grounds, which had been lent by the owner of White Hall to Mr. Honeyman. The sports had now commenced, for be it known, a picnic is not a picnic without the sports. These sports generally consisted of Foot Races, Obstacle Races, Jumping, High Jump and Low Jump, sometimes Horse Races, and other interesting and manly events. You pay a small entrance fee and, if you win the race or event, you get a prize provided by the giver of the picnic.

In this picnic of Mr. Honeyman's there were quite a number of events and the prizes were such as to excite intense desire and envy of the young men and women, for of course there were a couple of events for girls, races, etc. The prizes were of great variety, White Shirts, Coloured Shirts, Belts, Watches, Knives, Needle Cases etc.; but the prize was undoubtedly a pig, a live pig; and the event for which the pig was the prize was the most interesting and exciting, and yet most simple. All one had to do was to pay a sixpence for entering, then try and catch the pig by its greased tail; the first person that caught it properly and firmly got the pig.

At half past three the Gibsons arrived and were met at the gate by Thomas who insisted on paying for Susan and Ann's tickets, so gaining a point from the teacher who had not arrived yet. Miss Ann, who looked even more charming than usual, gave Thomas a shy smile that might have meant anything. As a matter of fact Miss Ann had not made up her mind yet which to take. She liked Thomas much better than the teacher, but the latter's dignity of position and comfortable circumstances still influenced her mind. Thomas who was going to partake in some of the sports, had left his gaiters at home, and was now wearing brilliant blue stockings, with brown shoes. The three passed through the gate, into the grounds and stood up watching a foot race which was being run. Just, as the race was ended in a tremendous burst of cheers and noise, Mr. Green rode up to them looking most important and affable on his young and small horse which was prancing and curvetting in a stylish way. When he saw Thomas with the girls, his face darkened a little, but it cleared almost at once, and dismounting he was gallant graciousness itself. "I am very glad you have managed to come and shed your pleasant influence on the scene to-day Miss Ann!" said he, "I don't know how I come so late. The reports of the school that I was writing, has delayed me."

The next foot race was one in which Thomas was going in for, so he left Ann and Susan in Mr. Green's charge and went off to do his best. During the race, Mr. Green carried off the girls to have ice cream and cakes, and when Thomas amidst tremendous clamour won the race, and a watch at the same time, the girls were absent eating their cakes. Putting on his shoes again he took the watch, and after a little looking found them. Mr. Green received him with a condescending and affable smile, "I am glad you have obtained the victory Thomas!" and Ann said shyly, "Ah glad you win Thomas" and asked to see the watch. Thomas was more than proud.

"You deserve a drink for that race," said Mr. Green. "What will you tek, a syrup or a kola?"

Thomas, who did not see why he should not benefit at the teacher's expense, answered readily:–

"Me tink me wi tek a kola, tank you sah!"

Mr. Green ordered a kola and Thomas drank it off in one breath.

When the girls had finished their ice cream and cakes,

Mr. Green paid up, rattling the loose money in his pocket incidentally as he put his hand in, and they all went out to see and enjoy what was going on. "You no going in for de next race Sue?" asked Thomas.

Susan nodded, "Yes, me believe me going. Ah really tink ah might ah try."

"You doan bring you entrance money yet?" said Thomas.

"No," said Susan, "me doan bring it yet."

"Dats alright den," said Thomas, "I wi pay fe it."

"Tenk you Thomas," said Susan, "It kine o' you an' ah mus' really try fe win."

So when the next race came on, Susan having her entrance money paid, took her place with the other girls, to run. The distance to run was shorter than that for the boys and men. And the girls did almost as quick running as the men. Urged on by Thomas and Ann's shouts, Susan ran as hard as she could but she was a little short-winded and only came in third. She got a small prize however, so she was not much disappointed.

"You warn fe eat less," said Ann, with a sister's frankness, "you too stout."

"Too stout wha?" said Susan, "as ah jus' going win, me breat kine o' fail me and I have fe go slower mek ah only get third."

Several interesting events then took place and all were

enjoying themselves. At about half-past four Mr. Honeyman announced in a loud voice that the pig race would now come off, and would everybody join in please – only 6d an entry.

After some hesitation several young men entered, including Thomas who saw in the pig perhaps an addition to the property he might possess with Ann.

When Mr. Honeyman had got ten entries and no more seem to be coming, he cleared the ground and prepared to let go the pig. First of all however, he placed the ten young men in a line, and at a distance of ten yards at right angles to opposite the middle man, he placed the pig. Mr. Green, who stood near the man and near the pig was to give the signal. Everybody and everything was ready, so lifting up his hand, Mr. Green said, "One! Two! Three!" and dropped a handkerchief. Immediately Mr. Honeyman let go the pig and immediately the young men started after it. The pig was not exactly fat and rather in good training being lean and muscular, and long and narrow, with a well greased tail. Now the fun and excitement began. The pig first of all, ran away from the men, then being headed, ran this way and that. One or two grabbed the tail, but couldn't grasp it firmly, and away the pig bolted, in and out among the spectators. Here and there it ran, twisting this way and that, squealing and causing some tumbles as people jumped and got out of the way. Thomas kept well after the pig, but did not try after its tail, knowing that it would be too greasy at first. After about five minutes of intense enjoyment to the crowd, the thing happened which finally decided Miss Ann in her choice of husband and gave Thomas a pig and a wife. The pig had come by this time round to its original position and was getting a little bit tired and going slower, was hard pressed indeed, for three young men were almost on him. Now it must be mentioned that just near here, there was a large stone with a small piece of naked and dirty land at the edge of which the teacher was standing and looking on with a dignified smile. As the foremost of the young men started forward to grab, the pig, with a last despairing effort, made a bolt at right angles and ran by Mr. Green. Mr. Green in getting out of the way stumbled against the stone and fell heavily on the pig and in the red and dirty patch of ground. A tremendous shout of cheers and laughter went up, especially magnified when it was seen that Thomas taking advantage of the pig being nearly squeezed to death by the teacher, had grabbed the tail firmly and in fact had won the prize. Mr. Green slowly rose to his feet, covered with red dust all over his face and shirt. He began to smile in a sickly way at first, but as he heard the shouts and laughter on all sides, his face got darker and darker. The black race loves a joke like this.

"Hi, Miser Green, you mus' ah sorry you no enter fur de race. You would ah get de pig," yelled one.

"Hi, no man!" said another, "De pig get him." Everybody was laughing and shouting, including Susan and Ann who shook with enjoyment of the joke. At the moment that the teacher went down, strange to say, Ann knew that she would accept Thomas and could never the teacher. Mr. Green must have felt something of this, for he walked past them without speaking, in a violent rage, and remounting his horse, rode home. Ann saw him go without any regret and it was a beautiful smile that lit her comely black face, when Thomas came up later to receive her words of congratulation.

LORITA (1905)

(By E. A. DODD, NEWPORT.)

CHAPTER I.

For some years the "backra" house at Hilltop had had as its sole occupants an old lady, the mistress and owner of Hilltop, and Teresa, the old nurse. Of feeble intellect in her old years, Miss Brown had had scarcely anything to do with the management of the property. Teresa, faithful with the faith of many years' service in the Brown family, had looked after her in every way, for though as old as Miss Brown herself, she was still strong and active. The two had subsisted on what little the place produced – a little coffee, a little pimento, a little rent and a little breadfruit. Taking good years and bad years, it was fair comfort, and Teresa had saved a few pounds for her mistress and put it in the bank in Kingston.

Then Miss Brown died, and a lawyer living some miles away and holding her will, wrote to a young man in England, named Digby Pallatt, that his distant cousin, Miss Brown, had left him Hilltop and a few pounds in the bank in Kingston.

Pallatt wrote back saying that he was very glad to hear that he had been left some property, as he had none or very little of his own, and that he was coming out by the steamer to take possession.

In the meantime McGiffey, the headman, who had practically managed the property for the last ten or twelve years, waited with some anxiety for Pallatt's coming. Not without some little honesty, he had refrained from using to the full the power he had had of making money out of Hilltop for himself, while his mistress would know nothing about it. He had contented himself with a large percentage of the crops and rents, and for one thing he kept off squatters. Yet he would have been more than human if he did not wax prosperous, so that he could get drunk every Saturday night and dress and live well. He waited, therefore, his new master's arrival with some anxiety, hoping that the latter would not notice nor enquire into the books and accounts of past crops, and that he would be kept on, for, as he muttered in his black beard with an oath, he meant to give trouble if he was not.

Pallatt arrived finally, and being a young man of considerable tact and insight into character, kept on McGiffey. He had a little capital, and he resolved to clean and stock, if not the whole, yet a good part of Hilltop, which he found nearly all in bush; keeping a few pounds for living expenses, he would trust to hard work and a land of abundant faithfulness.

It was two or three weeks before he saw Lorita. He had noticed McGiffey's cottage which stood just inside the entrance gate of the property. It did not belong to McGiffey, who had another house some distance away in the district, but he had lived there up to now, because it was convenient to him as headman, and Miss Brown had given him permission to do so.

The cottage itself lay in a glory of hibiscus. A large tree of the magnificent double red variety leant affectionately against the further end from the road, and passing round, swept the top of Lorita's door. All about the cottage, the red flowers stood bravely out of green and glossy leaves. They hedged with beauty a small garden in the front, and the coffee-piece back and front of the house. McGiffey, who had an eye for the picturesque, let them grow, and Lorita tended and pruned them carefully.

One morning in November, a bright and fair morning, Lorita, peeling some yams, heard the voice of some one singing and coming down the road towards the gate. She moved to the corner of the house nearer to see. Presently a young man whom she knew to be Pallatt, for she had seen him before, came riding over the slight hill down towards the gate. He rode easily and well. His head was thrown back, his body straight. His hazel eyes smiled with the morning light in them. Lorita could hear his fresh, sweet voice distantly:—

"So what care I tho' death be nigh,

I'll live for love or die,

So what care I though death be nigh,
I'll live for love or die."[133]

Lorita, half hidden by an orange tree, gazed as if entranced. Something rose in her throat that choked her, and she felt her bosom swell, as if it seemed to burst. Never had she seen anything as fair and wondrous as the careless and happy grace of the young man riding in the morning.

Just before he reached the gate, he stopped singing,

---

[133] This refrain is from *St. George and the Dragon,* a short story by Robert Grant. It was included in *Law-breakers and other stories* published by Scribner's in 1906 but was probably featured in a periodical, and read by Eddie, a year or two before when he was writing *Lorita.*

and Lorita, moved by a sudden impulse, ran down barefooted and opened the gate.

"Thank you," said Pallatt, riding through and looking at her anxiously and thinking that she looked very nice and picturesque. Her hair was black and straight and was bound under by a red handkerchief. Her face was olive and healthy and delicately shaped. Her eyes also, as she raised them for an instant, were dark and intelligent, and her lips were red. Pallatt noticed with approval that she wore a fresh clean gown of a yellow brown colour that fitted her slim little figure well.

"Thank you," he said again. "Are you McGiffey's daughter?"

"Yes sir!" The answer came shyly, yet distinctly, in a soft voice.

"Lovely lot of hibiscus you have there," said he. He went on round a bend of the road and was lost to view.

Lorita sprang lightly up the path back to the cottage and resumed her task. Her heart beat fast and she felt strangely excited. As she would have put it, she felt funny. A magnetic personality seemed to be in the air, and the red flowers above her head were undoubtedly a richer red and more beautiful.

McGiffey was the son of a white gentleman and a dark woman. He, McGiffey, in his ignorance it is to be supposed, spoke of his mother as a nice lady and never called his father a gentleman. He saw very little of him, however, as Mr. McGiffey, a man of no little learning and parts, lived chiefly in England, where he died when his son was young man. McGiffey married a white girl, the daughter of a white emigrant, and had only one child, Lorita. His wife died when the child was ten years old, having taught Lorita first how to read and write. Lorita henceforth associated with Miss Brown and Teresa, who gave her a lot of advice.

She read a great deal for, strangely, a good deal of her grandfather had entered into her, which showed itself in her keeping to herself and filling her fancy with thoughts derived from books at Hilltop. Her father scarcely understood her, but was fond of her. The people and neighbours in the district thought her half simple, but more than half clever. The fact that she never went to school, that she had no brother or sister, that Miss Brown and Teresa looked after her, that her father though bad in some ways, obtruded none of his badness on her – all these facts kept her, if not innocent of all evil around her, yet innocent and free of evil herself.

That evening, when the lamps or rather lamp was lit, Digby, after his simple dinner had his usual chat with Teresa who kept house and did nearly everything for him. Digby as a boy had spent two years in Jamaica so he was familiar enough with their way of living and speech.

"Teresa," said he, "I saw the girl, McGiffey's daughter to-day. She opened the gate for me."

Teresa grunted. "She open the gate for you?"

"Yes," said Pallatt, "she ran down and opened it as I was riding through. She is a nice looking girl and for a wonder she was clean and nicely dressed."

"Then why should she not be nicely dressed and clean?" asked the old woman turning round. "I can tell you Miser Digby dat it is not only backra can clean and dress." Digby was amused secretly, for he knew that Teresa was proud and touchy on some points.

"Oh, I know that," he said calmly, "but it is strange I have never seen her before. Does she ever come up here?"

"Come up yah?" asked Teresa, "Before you come, she used to be up yah ebery day an read book and talk with me. I love her fe true."

"What's her name?"

"She name Lorita, Lorita McGiffey."

"She reads books, eh?"

"Yes, sah. She read book jus' like you or any backra. Sometimes I think she is half simple, but she really not so. She is daughter of nearly white people? she nuh mus' favour backra?"

"H'm" grunted Digby. Shortly after he went to bed, but did not dream of Lorita; he dreamt instead of a girl in England, and thought he saw her standing daintily amid a glory of red flowers and green leaves.

CHAPTER II.

Pallatt, a few days before he saw Lorita, had scored a victory over McGiffey by sheer tact and personality. He had, for more than one reason, refrained from enquiring too closely into the latter's past stewardship and his accounts of crops and moneys of Hilltop. He had however spoken firmly to McGiffey, told him that he liked him, and instead of percentages would give him instead a fixed salary or wages per month, with a few privileges. It was more than fair for him, a headman, but it was much lower than what McGiffey was accustomed to make out of the place, and it meant more work; still there was a look in Pallatt's eye which made him think well of it. So being in truth fond of the place and liking Pallatt, he consented, and proved as faithful and as hardworking as a man of his stamp and education could be expected to be.

"Oh, McGiffey!" said Pallatt to him as he was going home after his day's work; "I wish you would give me a few slips of that double red Hibiscus at your cottage, I want them in my garden."

"Right, sah!" said McGiffey. "I wi cut as much as you want. In fac, I wi mek Lorita, me daughter, carry dem up and plant dem in de garden fe you. She understan' such ting."

"All right," said Pallatt, "thank you!"

The next evening, – it was two days after she opened the gate for Pallatt – Lorita appeared with a lot of slips. She looked bright and pleased. Pallatt went with her into the garden which he was getting into order against certain happy days in the future, and ordered Sam, a diminutive but old boy of large and cheerful countenance, to bring his hoe. Pallatt had found him with the name of Hezekiah Jehosophat Wylie, but to save time as he explained to him, he called him Sam.

"You see, Lorita," said Pallatt, "I want the slips planted around the garden near the fence to make a sort of hedge."

"Yes, sir," said Lorita. "You show me, and I wi' plant dem."

Pallatt showed her, and Lorita planted away. When the planting was done he called her into Teresa's room and made the old woman cut her a piece of cake. He offered it to her nicely as some men have a way of doing and she accepted it.

"Oh, Lorita," said he, "I hear you like reading, and that you used to come up and see Teresa often."

Lorita blushed.

"Well," continued he, "don't let me interfere with you. Come up and see Teresa as often as you wish and I will lend you a couple of books. I am very fond of books myself so I understand why you like it."

"Yes sir; thank you, sir," she answered shyly, yet not ungracefully.

Two days later she came up to see Teresa and sat in the latter's room a long time. She read a book occasionally and more often looked out of the window at Pallatt in the distant cow pen, his jacket off and his face bronzed and alight with the sun. She went out later and watered the slips, and Pallatt came up and thanked her for doing so. Her simplicity and manner, so much removed from her own class in life, interested him. "By James!" he muttered to himself, as he looked at Lorita going home in the distance, straight and graceful as a dart. "She's a fine and very unusual sort of girl.

Fancy her reading novels and liking them. I don't know what's going to happen to her."

This was the beginning of life to Lorita. She looked after the slips herself and they grew apace. She brought up fruit of all sorts for Pallatt asking, from some innate thought, a small price for them. Pallatt was very kind to her, showing in his manner, however, that he was a good master and she of the servant class. Not that he was not anything but entirely courteous and polite to her. Yet it was enough for her to run and open the gate for him. She did not know that she was in love with him. She did not think of such a thing. He was a 'buckra' and far above her, yet thanks be to God he was a very honourable young man and a gentleman. She only knew that she would have given him anything, honour and all, and thought it right too. And in truth the sin, if sin had been incurred, would not have been hers. Yet even of an evening the choking feeling would rise in her throat and her bosom swell with her soul's unconscious desire for something it had not nor could ever have.

One afternoon, late enough, a few months after, she was peeling and putting her father's simple dinner to boil, when she saw a young man open the gate and ride in up the path towards her. She recognised Stephen Hoffner, a shopkeeper and speculator living at the small village two or three miles away. He rode up to the house and dismounted. His face was amiable and fat. He was very fat and soft looking. His hair was sleek and black, his complexion pink and white like a woman's. His eyes were also black and he showed his teeth when he smiled. It was obvious that he had some Jewish blood in him. Deceit and sensuality were written large on him.

"Evening, Miss Lorita," he said pleasantly, showing his teeth.

Lorita looked at him and said gravely, "Evenin'."

"You farder is not in?" said Hoffner.

"No," said Lorita. "He is at de house."

"Well, I did want to see him," said Hoffner; "but it can stay." He continued after a pause, "And you is better company."

Lorita took no notice. Hoffner came closer. "How would you like fe prepare dinner fe me Miss Lorita?" said he, his evil face grinning seductively; "you is jus de gal for me."

Lorita continued silent, and calmly went on with her work though her fingers trembled nervously and indignantly. "Tell me nuh," continued Hoffner. "Mek me marry. You is a pretty gal you know, and I really love you. Tell me nuh!"

Lorita was still silent, so Hoffner finally came closer and stretched forth his arm to put around her waist. "Gimme a kiss," said he; "Dere is nobody aroun'."

Lorita gave a sort of short cry as he touched her, and suddenly lifting a pan of pig's feeding near her, full of pot water and peelings, flung it hard at Hoffner, then rushed quickly into her room and barred the door.

The pan struck Hoffner's hat with some force, knocking it off and the dirty water and peelings ran over his face and coat. He swore loudly in a hot rage and did his best to wipe himself clean with his handkerchief.

"Arlright Miss Lorita," shouted he to the closed door. "You prefer buckra like Massa Pallatt, ehm? You wi' sorry fe dis yah, you -----." Here he uttered vile obscene words and oaths, his fat face evil with passion.

Through the jealousies Lorita saw him presently go to his horse and mount and ride away. Then she came out later, but did not go up to the house as her wont, nor did she tell her father of Hoffner's conduct, fearing he might do something rash in his temper. She felt troubled however, and excited.

That same evening Hoffner at his shop spread craftily a horrible and vile slander about Lorita and Pallatt.

CHAPTER III.

The day after, McGiffey came out to the village and Hoffner perceived from the latter's behaviour to him that Lorita had told nothing to her father. He then resolved to create mischief, for he thought that the headman did not like Pallatt. Into McGiffey's ears he poured the slander he had spread, asserting it was true.

McGiffey heard him to the end silently enough though his eyes blazed. "My God, Misser Hoffner!" said he finally. "If it not true what you seh, and I doan believe it yet, I will kill you." With this he turned away. Hoffner began to repent of going so far.

McGiffey went straight to Hilltop, and in an interview with Pallatt told him everything that Hoffner had said. Pallatt listened quietly, then said, "If I did not believe that you were doing what you thought right, McGiffey, I would knock you down for asking me such a question, but on my honour every word is a d---d lie. Do you believe me?"

"Yes, sah," said McGiffey, "I believe you."

"But McGiffey," said Pallatt, as the latter was going away, "let me manage Hoffner, you hear."

Two days later Hoffner was walking past Pallatt's place on a lower road with a comrade of his, an evil living and weak looking young man. The two were chatting away, when they met Pallatt coming round the corner in his shirt sleeves and a short cow-skin whip in his hand. They were passing him keeping up their loud laughter, when Pallatt stopped Hoffner.

"Hoffner, a few words with you." Hoffner paused.

Pallatt looked pale and a slight smile was on his lips. "I believe you told McGiffey a lie about me and his daughter, didn't you?" Hoffner thought he looked frightened and answered with an impertinent laugh, "Well Misser Pallatt, all young man is alike and maybe it not so lie."

Suddenly with an exclamation, Pallatt sprang on him and holding him by the collar in a grip like a vice, brought down his whip across the fat brute till his trousers were cut in pieces and his body bled. The other young man did not interfere from reasons of cowardice. Pallatt flogged the howling and weeping Hoffner till the latter was nearly senseless, then flung him into the middle of the road. "Go home, you dirty brute," said he, his voice trembling, "and don't repeat a word of what you said."

Hoffner picked himself up groaning, and casting a very evil look at Pallatt staggered with his friend around a corner.

Some days after Lorita was with Teresa talking. Pallatt had spoken more kindly to her than ever and she was feeling happy. "Lorita," said Teresa suddenly, "Missa Digby going married one of dese days you know; he engage to one girl in England. Him ever tell you?"

Lorita turned a little pale, and said faintly, "No."

"Well ah true," said the old woman not looking at her, "Him hab him photograph, or sich ting hang up in him room."

Lorita answered not; the room seemed to have got darker and there was a sudden dull pain in her breast. She hardly said anything to the old woman's rambling words and took her leave early. The pain grew more intense as she reached home and saw the hibiscus flowers flirting gaily in the sunshine. She went inside but she could not rest, the pain in her heart grew and grew till she felt she could shriek aloud. So she wandered down over the commons aimlessly towards the lower road. She went over the wall scarcely knowing what she was doing and went along the road which was hedged rather thickly and not much used. Was it a strange power or fate that she met Hoffner presently? He was slightly the worse for drink, but his eyes lightened as he beheld Lorita who came towards him almost unconscious of his presence.

"Ah, Miss Lorita," said he with a smile. "You treat me like a dog de oder day ehm? I wi' get me kiss to-day doh."

He caught her firmly by the arm as she was passing him, and tried to draw her to him. She struggled violently and shrieked out for help, loudly and clearly in the still air. Hoffner still struggled with her, but he was gaining the mastery of her and brought her face near his. Presently a horse came at full gallop round the road and Pallatt rode up towards them. Hoffner turned round, letting go Lorita and pulled out a revolver. "Don't come near, or I wi shot you dead," he yelled out. "Keep off."

Pallatt heeded not but jumped off his horse and rushed forward. Lorita saw the revolver in Hoffner's hand and sprang on his arm and clutched the weapon with her own hand, bending it down. There was a sharp report. Lorita staggered back with her hand to her breast and a little cry. Pallatt caught her in his arms and bore her gently to the bank, still keeping his arms about her. Hoffner went to the horse and jumping on his back galloped off and was never seen by Pallatt again.

Lorita lay in Pallatt's arms with her eyes closed and blood trickled from her breast and crimsoned the frock. By a strange coincidence a solitary hibiscus grew by the wall just over their heads and its red flowers seemed to stoop towards her in pity. Presently she opened her eyes. "I never meant to do it, but I pulled the trigger myself," she said faintly, "not him. But," she continued with an effort, "it all for the better. I glad it turn out so. Good-bye Misser Digby." Then more faintly still, "Good-bye Digby." She closed her eyes as if exhausted, then opened them wide and said in the strangest, sweetest little voice, "I'll live for love or die, I'll live for love or die." And with that she turned her head on Digby's arm and died.

* * * * * * *

So it was for the better. She had everything against her, for the time was not yet come, and death was all her promise and her hope. Truly the white man's burden is great, for it is of his own fashioning.

FARDER MATNEY'S PIGS (1909)

By E. A. Dodd.

"Marnin! Cousin Will!"

"Hi! marnin! Sah!"

Cousin Will and Mr. Sam "Simit" shook hands gravely in the middle of the road; the process of salutation being of a slow peculiar sort different from the quick and present method of shaking hands. Cousin Will, whose real name was William Riley, but who went by the other name with his friends, then inquired after Mr. Smith's "farmbly."

"Dem tan well enuf sah" answered Mr. "Simit" in a gloomy tone, "De times is not too hard, and the corn crop come out well enuf."

"Ah glad fe hear it," replied Cousin Will. "But top! me no tink me see you pass long ah go up in de district jus now? You come back quick?"

"Yes sah," replied Mr. "Simit", "you did seh me, but me tun back; for as ah could ah catch by de Chineeman shop, dis buoy Garge Meikle call me seh ah mus' come up ah Farder Matney, if I warn see him before him dead, as him really bad."

"My eh!" said Cousin Will sympathetically. "Ah sorry fe hear it. Dey mus ah sen' fe call you?!"

"Yes sah," answered Mr. Smith. "So I tun straight back an' ah jus' going change me shut and den go up guh see him."

"Yes sah; den ah wun stop you," answered Cousin Will, moving out of the way of Mr. Simit's donkey; then he added:

"But ah really true dat him bad? him so often sick to deat dat maybe after all wen you go up dey you we fine him a chaw him little piece of nagur yam."

"Oh doan talk a wud lik dat, sah," replied Mr. Simit reprovingly to Cousin Will's smile. "Him bad dis time to deat's door."

Cousin Will who was rather a humourist hastened to assure him of the goodness of his intentions.

"Oh, ah doan mean nuttin' by dat sah!" So he said, "but him sick, and you might ah eben seh dead, so often dat ah kine ah tink him ah mek fool o' people jus' out o' sport." Then as Mr. Simit moved off without answering he added, "Ah no tink you is de neares' relation to him? Tell you what Sam, dem two little pig up ah Farder's would ah set you up well fe married. Wheh you tink?"

Mr. Simit saw no joke in the situation however, being anxious about the future possession of the pigs, he touched up the donkey to a quicker pace, leaving the highly amused Cousin Will with a stern "Oh doan speak a wud like dat sah" that only added to Cousin Will's laughter.

On reaching home a few minutes later Mr. Simit hastily tied out his donkey and changed into his Sunday clothes. This transformation took very little time, and before long he was approaching the house and yard of Farder Matney, his uncle.

The hurry and anxiety displayed by Mr. Sam Simit to reach his uncle, would certainly have given the latter much surprise and pleasure, if he could have seen his devotion. Unfortunately, Farder Matney could not see it and, perhaps after, he would not have put down the anxiety to devotion alone; it being but human to be suspicious of affection. Mr. Simit passed on his way one or two women dressed gayly and cheerfully in their best garments who were also going up to see Farder Matney before his demise. To these he gave a sympathetic nod and salutation and hurried on. As he entered the yard, he beheld a saddled horse tied to a tree by the house, which trifling event seemed to annoy Mr. Simit. "Garge got him horse. Him can get yah firs'! de crabbitch fellow!" he muttered. "But mek him wait, four foot nuh ketch train all time." With this philosophic thought he passed into the doorway and beheld his brother George seated by the bed on which lay the dying Mr. Matney.

It may be well to explain here that Ole Farder Matney had been sick off and on for the past two years with a chronic complaint, which had frequently brought him very low; so low once or twice that his nearest relatives, George and Sam "Simit" who had been disappointed about his death on these occasions were becoming rather impatient over their uncle's sickness. A feeling of rivalry, hidden for the time by the respect which the lower classes have even more than the upper for the laughter of their neighbours, existed between George and Sam.

George was a teacher and better off than Sam, who therefore thought that he should get the greater part of Mr. Matney's belongings at the latter's death, and he especially determined to get hold of a pair of young pigs – the same that Cousin Will had spoken of. George in his turn reasoned in his mind that as the elder and as one who had a high dignity of position to keep up, he should get the most *with* the pigs. It was with some of the bitterness arising from this rivalry that Sam gazed on George, who as teacher and a catechist had taken upon himself the task of helping the old man through the dark gates with words of religion.

On seeing Sam in the doorway, George held up his hand as a sign for quiet, at the same time nodding his welcome. To his brother's hoarse whisper as to how their uncle was, he replied in a slightly less hoarse whisper that "Him was very bad; weak fe tru," at which a gloomy satisfaction seemed to spread over their faces.

The house in which the master lay dying was of the simplest in design and size. It had only one room, which room had one small window and one door. The window was of the kind that cannot be opened, and indeed was not built for the purpose of ventilation but as an ornament. The door of course was the means by which Mr. Matney entered his bedroom and had to be opened sometimes. At night, however, it was well closed to prevent any air at all coming in. From which facts it will be seen that Mr. Matney must have been a strong man in some ways. The room itself was fairly large, being about twelve feet square. The bed which was of wood – wooden lathes across wooden supports with a grass mattress on top – occupied one corner with its foot to the door. Near the door was a wooden bench, and there was besides a stiff and hard mahogany chair of the usual square pattern. On this, by the way was George seated. A barrel occupied another corner and there were various shelves and nails and pegs about, which supported his crockery, earthenware jugs, glasses, etc., clothes, whips and such like. Sam took his seat on the bench and, with two women inside and a couple others outside around the door, prepared to listen to his brother's comforting texts. The master of the house, who lay on the bed on his back in a sort of stupor, was a man of about sixty years of age. Around one temple was a rather dirty bandage and he lay silent with closed eyes; in truth he seemed very weak.

"Is your heart fix on Jesus, Farder?" asked George in a quiet tone.

Farder Matney turned his head slowly and answered in a weak husky voice, "Yes on Jesus Chris' de Sabiour."

"Do you really belieb dat him can save you Farder?" continued the teacher. There was a long pause, for the sick man could not gather his thoughts quickly; then he replied simply, "Yes."

"Dat's right farder" said his nephew, "If you want to save, you mus' believe dat Jesus Chris' die and rise for you and dat you repent of you sin." The old man was silent, save that he sighed or rather breathed heavily.

"Do you want me to sing you a nice hymn, about de Lord Jesus?" asked George after a pause. Farder Matney kept silent, and the teacher put the question again, and finally the old man answered in his husky and trembling voice: "Yes but not too loud."

A smile even passed over the faces of two of the women looking in at the door, for George was rather celebrated for his powerful voice, which indeed was the chief musical instrument in the choir. With an assuring "Arlright Farder," George opened his hymn book, and turning over the leaves finally fixed his choice on one with quiet and even chords. He read out the first verse distinctly, and then proceeded to sing it in a soft but rather curious key. Some allowance however must be made for a man who being accustomed to roar as it were as a lion, had now to murmur softly like a bird. George with perfect confidence and not a lot of embarrassment sung through the whole hymn, reading and singing the verses alternately. The room was exceedingly hot and it had its effect on George, who being rather stout perspired freely. It was a detail that Balzac would have loved. The drops of moisture on the reader's face every now and then fell on the open page with a loud splash. These obstructions he quietly wiped off with a dirty fore-finger and sung on. The hymn being finished George then knelt down and offered up a prayer for his soul.

George's prayer was long and rambling and in no way cohesive, but as it dealt chiefly with his uncle's sinfulness and the goodness of his Maker, it doubtless suited its purpose well enough.

Sam and the women looked on, and listened critically, like spectators of some scene of a play. George in finishing, rose more heated than ever, and pulling out a red silk handkerchief wiped his brow and face and inside his collar, and dusted his knees. Sam who was impatient at being inactive, then made a step towards his brother and whispered a few words to him. In answer George looked at his uncle, then comforted by the sameness of his appearance, got up and went outside with Sam. The two moved aside from the women, and stopped by a pig-sty near the house to talk.

"Him tell you anyting bout de house an' de thing dem?" asked Sam in a low tone, "who fe tek care a' dem when he gone?"

George shook his head. "Not a ting. Him never say a wud to me. In fac' him scarcely does seh a word except when I speak to him. Him jus' stay so; silent arl de time."

"Well fe de matter of dat," said Sam, "me and you is de only relative, an' it is but right dat we should look arter de tings dem."

"Ob course," agreed the teacher. "That's what him would like."

"But you tink him really bad?" asked Sam in an anxious tone as befitted a near relative.

George nodded. "Oh him really bad dis time! Neber see him so bad. Him take no physical nourishment since yesterday marnin' and him really weak. If he do die," continued George in a grave musing voice, "Well den, we not to complain. It is de Lord will. An' him been so long in pain dat may be, it will be just as well."

"You speak true sah," agreed Sam. "He suffer a long time."

George took two ripe bananas out of his pocket and offered one to his brother who took it thankfully.

"We scarcely did take any food dis mornin'," said he with an apologetic air. "So I just brought dese two bananas along in case of necessity."

"You right sah, you right," said Sam, peeling his banana. "Food is a ting, you carn do without it."

They chucked the skins in the direction of the sty for the benefit of the two precious young pigs that each was hoping to get possession of. One skin fell in the pen, and was eagerly devoured, and the other fell just outside.

The two brothers approached the sty and leaning against the fence discussed the merits of the pigs.

"You tink dem na grow?" said Sam admiringly. "Dat shoat is de very pig ah'd ah like fe get fe put in dat old sty ah hab ah yard."

"Dey growin fe true," agreed George. "I hab such a pile of feeding' o' home, ah don't know what fe do wi ih."

Each brother knew what was in the other's mind, but was too cautious to show his knowledge.

Presently George remarked that, "We better guh back as the old man was critical" and must want his help.

They turned back and took the seats they had before; George first of all examining his uncle to see if he were any worse. His examination consisted in holding up the patient's wrist with one hand while he gravely put his forefinger on the sinews of the wrist where he could not feel the pulse. It was a position of dramatic effect and aroused the admiration of Sam. George after a minute or two then put down the limp wrist and shook his head forebodingly. "How you feel, Fader?" He asked of the old man. "You feel weak?"

There was no reply. Silent and still the old man lay

with closed eyes. "You nuh got any ting to give him?" asked Sam leaning forward. "Him really look bad."

"Me tink we had better give him a little whiskey, sah," said his brother. "It will raise up him spirit."

Sam nodded. It was curious to see the five or six spectators all waiting patiently in their best clothes on the spirit of a man – to see it leave the body. And it is sad but true, they were all more or less patient from feelings of inquisitiveness and interest.

Very shortly after the two brothers had left the sty, one of the pigs smelt the attractive aroma from the banana skin, which had fallen just outside the sty. That aroused a great longing in the pig's breast. He grunted and walked about the sty, expressing his longing, and always coming back to the same spot, near the fence. He then tried the fence, shoving his nose through a slit, he pushed hard. The slit widened. He shoved harder and harder. It widened more. Then he gave a grand and final push and was outside with a scramble. The skin was eaten with relish, and lawfully the pig should then have gone back into his sty. This however did not suit the pig and he wandered towards the house. There surely, must be more banana skins around. The shoat seeing her brother go out promptly followed and after making sure that only the smell of the skin was left, also wandered away.

Unluckily for the pigs, however, a small boy came along. His name was Hezekiah Timkins, and he was employed by "Farther Matney" as a help of all sorts; to feed the pigs, act as cook and do other like work. Seeing the pigs out, his soul was filled first with dismay; then with the spirit of action and pursuit he started after them, and after the boar particularly. They immediately bolted in opposite directions. A pig does not run in a way calculated to make the spectator think that he is running for any particular goal. On the contrary, he runs in a mad fashion, twisting and bolting in short straight lines, for he does not think of going round an object that he can possibly knock over or jump over, no matter what it be. This is the way the boar that Hezekiah was pursuing frantically ran and was hard to catch. The chase went into the coffee patch, then round the sty and straight towards the house. At this moment Sam, who had heard the noise, came out and seeing the pig coming towards him, waited till he was quite close and then made a grab at him. He missed of course and immediately the pig bolted through the open door and into the room knocking over a bench. Father Matney had once or twice when he was stronger fed the pigs in the room at the entrance, so they were accustomed to look on it as a place of good things. George on seeing the pig grabbed him by the leg as he ran almost against him, and at once that pig emitted an appalling squeal. The effect on Father Matney was wonderful. He started up and rolled over on his side unwittingly. The bed unfortunately was too narrow and before George could catch him, he had dropped off the bed on the floor hitting his head. One of the women in the room gave out a startled "Lord me massa, him mus' a dead." George let go the pig and helped by Sam who had come in lifted the old man back on the bed. He was groaning and, strange to say, his extreme look of lifelessness had gone. It was then seen that the abscess on his left temple had burst lifting as it were the weight which produced the torpor.

George looked at Sam with a curious air. "Ah do

believe as the abscess break him stans a chance of recovery."

Sam said nothing then, but he went presently and catching hold of Hezekiah he administered to that howling youth a severe castigation; giving as a reason his carelessness for disturbing Farder Matney by letting the pig into the room.

Some months after this, on the day before Christmas a crowd of women and men were gathered around Father Matney's house. A fine pig had just been killed by the master of the house, and he was selling out the pork to would be buyers. The master himself, looking quite well and strong for an old man, was much affected at the killing of the pig. "Yes Sah, ah love dat pig fe true. It was dat pig dat sabe me life. "Doctor"! ah guh to doctor, ah any good? Ah try arl sort of medecin: dey neber do me any good. Ah try dis an' ah try dat, ah jus' de same except dat ah little worse. Ah jus' a deat door. Marse George yah eber pray ober me, ah try tek me soul ah shove it into heaven, an' den de pig sabe me."

All the spectators were interested especially Cousin Will, who had taken over the task of cutting up and selling the pork for Mr. Matney. He had a smile on his face and the smile broadened into a laugh which forced him to drop the knife when Sam with a long grave face came up to buy "four poun' a' pourk." Sam grew impatient at Cousin Will's laughter,

"Ah, stop you laugh sah, and gie me de pourk, ah in hase, an' want guh," he said very angrily.

Cousin Will laughed more, then finally controlled his voice. "Ah comin', sah; ah comin'. Now you want four poun'? Tell you what, Sam, de pig really sweet, you know;

mek ah gie you ten poun'. You nah want it? Oh well den see, yah, tek de four poun', ah tink ah know why you nuh want more." Sam took his pork in severe silence and departed without a word.

MR. "SIMITT" CORN (1910)[134]

(AN ECHO OF THE DROUGHT IN SOUTH MANCHESTER)

On the bare red spot in front of a two roomed hut on the Southern Hills a little negro boy stood gazing listlessly across to the hill side opposite. He leant against a half tumbled fence post, and the attitude showed up his dirty torn shirt, and a miserable remnant of a pair of trousers.

It was nine o'clock of an October morning. The sun shone brightly, too brightly, on a soil parched and famished by drought and strong winds. A few days past, a shower of rain had fallen, and the grateful earth had shown a slight, but alas! passing change of colour in the roots of what was once grass.

Yet the month was October, everyone hoped for more rain, and with the hope of it, Stephen "Smitt," the shopkeeper, at the neighbouring Cross Roads, was planting out a quarter of an acre of the hillside opposite "Miss Reid's" with corn. Sam Reid, leaning against the post, watched Mr. Smitt dropping the corn, three grains at a time, into each little hole dug with a cutlass in the hard dry ground. He scratched his right foot, with a toe of his left, and duly took an interest in the scene before him. He was hungry "fe true," but he displayed no restlessness over it; he knew quite well there was nothing to eat in the house, not even a piece of bammy, and it was vainer to look on the coffee patch where a few bananas still stood stunted and yellow. His little stomach was thin and straight – Time was, when what with yam and sweet potatoes

---

[134] 'Smitt', of course, is the Jamaican pronunciation of 'Smith'.

and bananas and fruit, it was round and prominent and his skin was black and smooth – Now grey and dry he was thin as a stick and his face was old – too old –

His father had disappeared under the stress of the drought nine months back, and his mother had kept herself and him and Lucy – his sister a little older than himself – by the little money they had got from pimento picking and a little occasional washing.

Suddenly on Sam's dull ear came the sound of his mother's voice from the hut. She was speaking to herself in a loud plaint, as is the custom of the negroes, – "My God! Yes! Miser Smitt can plant him corn, and fatten 'pon it – an why! Sake o' de ting him get from we poor nagar who had to gie'm all we have to buy de flour an' salt ting to keep we body an' soul togeder! – Ah had tree pig, six foul, and two goat last year dis' time, and weh dem dey? Fus, ah sell dis one to pay Mr. Smitt for what I owe for flour! And den I sell dat, and den he seh him goin' levy, and ah sell two, and so dem gone! An' de price of the flour! Lord me Gawd! when I tink dat when him know we have to buy, him raise de price o' de cornmeal instead of him lower! Lord! It mek me blood bwoil! an ah mad! Massa God will punish him, doh."

There was silence a while and then – "And me poor pickney dem! Since yesterday middle day one gill bammy for de two of dem! Dem wi' dead sure! an' if ah should ax Mr. Smitt for a little teeny handful o' de corn to go boil fe dem, him would a cus me, cus me! an yet my Gawd, him hab me pig, an' him hab me goat an' hab me fowl, an' him will tek me pickney next! I wish to Gawd, rat and mongoose will eat out him corn grain dem!" Silence again.

The first part of his mother's speech was wasted on Sam, who had heard it all often before, but the last part took his ear and brain. And for a while he cogitated, looking at Mr. Smitt across the dividing fence with more interest. Then he straightened himself and went to look for his sister who was somewhere at the back of the yard. Meanwhile Mrs. Reid put on a fairly clean and a fairly whole dress and went out on the road to go and beg for a pittance from the parson for herself and the children. There was a little money maybe coming at the end of the week, and she must try and get a little food even one bite a day till then.

. . . .

Five o'clock of the next morning, in the grey of another perfect day – In Mr. Smitt's new and freshly planted ground two small figures with crouched backs, moved and stopped, and moved and stopped with quick haste. They kept searching as it seemed, for something which they ever found and put in small "shut pans" that they carried. Yet their task took time and it was broad daylight with a risen sun, before they straightened and quickly sped over into Mrs. Reid's yard –

They had begun their work the last evening before, as the spot had been deserted by everyone around.

A little while later on, Lucy, the girl, took a large shut pan to her mother who was boiling a little hot water for a thin tea of old coffee and head-sugar. "See yah. Ma, boil dis corn fe me." She said simply –

Her mother turned and looked at the corn. "My Lord! what is this! chile, weh you get it?" She took the corn and

171

looked at it, and suddenly understood for there was red dirt on some of the grains. "You tek it nuh?" she cried sharply, "you tief it nuh?" Lucy bent her head, "Yes," she said sullenly, "I tief it from Mr. Smitt" – "You tief it, an' you nuh shame! Oh! my Gawd! She tief it an' no shame. Oh! my Gawd, dat dis should come on me!" The poor woman put down the corn, and burst out weeping and sobbed as if her heart would break.

Later on her sobs ceased and she dried her eyes and called Lucy who had crept away not understanding her mother's grief.

"Lucy," said her mother quietly, "mek up de fire; you do wrong, but ah can see you suffer, an' not a ting to eat. An' ah say, you Sam, bring the mortar yah!" "And if Miser Smitt (this to herself) ever come seh anything to me, bout tief – my Gawd. I will talk to him."

That night there was a heavy shower of rain and a week later Mr. Smitt coming to look for his blades of corn only beheld a few solitary examples on a bare open space. He exclaimed on it, till certain signs showed him what had happened and his rage broke forth only to be dispelled later on by the thought of the greatness of the necessity that drove his fellows to such extremities, that they could come and burrow for corn like the very rats of the earth.

E. A. D.

Jamaica.

THE OBEAH OF 'OLE SHAW' (1911)

A JAMAICA STORY

On the concrete edge of the tank the two boys sat with their legs hanging over the edge of the water. The elder and more intelligent looking of the two was a coloured lad, about as dark as an Italian, with a bright face. The other was of the dark brown of the ordinary negro. The two however, despite this difference in colour were of the same social degree, being both "boys" working on the pimento and coffee property of Cave Valley. They had come to look for mules that had been turned out to pasture. This pasture was rather large and being covered with clumps of woodland and scrub, the boys had not yet found them. They had resolved after some search, partly in a spirit of idleness, partly from experience, to wait at the tank until the mules should come out in the heat of the day to drink water. The fact that the tank was the water supply at once tells that the property was in the mountains. These tanks are universal in certain of the mountainous parts of Jamaica; and, there hardly ever being any thing like a drought, give a constant supply of pure rain water. The day was a lovely one. In the distance a semicircle of sea stretched beyond the far plains. A cool breeze blew continually. No wonder that the negro is gay and careless when the land he lives in conspires with might and main to make him so. The two boys chatted away, happy and idle. The conversation had turned to obeahism. "I neber see a man who like fe talk about obeah like Ole Shaw," said Will the elder. "You watch him Thomas when him come wid de gang here to eat breakfas', him will tell dem dis and tell dem dat, how powerful it is, an' what it can do."

"Oh, him believe in it, fe true," said Thomas, "him 'fraid of it, like him 'fraid o' debbil!"

"An what it is?" asked Will apostrophizingly. "It is pure nonsense. Most part of it. Lard, I larf till I nearly dead one time when me and him did ah trabbel late one ebening tru dis same pasture yah. It was jus' after dusk, but not properly dark wid de night yet. Same so, him was talking all sort of foolishness 'bout duppy and rolling calf an' him was well work up wid de thoughts o' dem. Well, when we was passing through dat little piece o' dark woodland down at de gully gate, you know where I mean?" Thomas nodded. "Him was walking a little 'head o' me and jus' as we ketch round de corner to come to de gate, dat white calf o' Marse George run pas' and we see it kine o' white. Well sah, as I see it so, I let go one piece of yell and bolt into de bush." Here Will lay back and laughed, while Thomas joined him in the loud laughter of the negro.

"Well mek I tell you Thomas," said Will recovering. "As I yell out so, Ole Shaw gie one single jump, and den cry out 'Lard, me God,' and run like de wind up de path and him neber stop running till him get to Marse Campbell shop, where him sleep de night."

"Ha, ha!" laughed Thomas. "Ha! Ha! You mus' a frighten too!"

"Well," said Will, "ah neber dream of turning frighten at first, for ob course I know de calf; but when I cry out so, de noise dat I mek and de noise dat Ole Shaw mek, frighten me one way, dat ah neber stop running till I get to de yard, where I laugh till I nearly dead. Ah hear afterwards, dat Ole

Shaw tell dem at de shop one wonderful story about how him see a rolling calf, white wid two eyes red like dem make out o' fire coal." "Ha, ha!" yelled the two boys. They both rolled back enjoying the joke heartily. After a while they were silent and Will gazed thoughtfully and half sleepily out towards the pimento trees that studded the common, looking handsome with their dark green leaves and white limbs.

"If ah could only fool him up wid some sort o' obeah," he said presently, "it would really sweet me."

"Dat is if he doant find it out!" said the more cautious Thomas.

Will turned his gaze on Thomas who had discarded an old tweed jacket he wore and now exhibited some torn shirt and some of his own dark skin in torn pants. An idea seemed to strike him. "Gimme dat jacket yah a little, Thomas!" said he.

"What for?" asked Thomas, handing it slowly over, however.

"You doan mind!" said Will, "I only want dis ole pocket lining, yah."

"What you want it for?" asked Thomas, who did not want to see his jacket despoiled.

"Nutten," said Will ambiguously, proceeding to tear out the lining; "If you wait jus' one minute, I wi' tell you."

Thomas looked on half sulkily as Will calmly took out the lining that formed the bag of the pocket.

"Now," said Will, "You see this bag, me buoy? Well, den dis is obeah! Dis is what going frighten Ole Shaw out o' him senses."

"How?" said Thomas, a little more interestedly.

"You jus' wait!" said Will, "I am going to fill it up wid some stuff, and Lard! you wait so see if it doan frighten him!"

Will jumped up and went through the rail fence that protected the tank from beasts that might drop in. Thomas followed under the spell of the superior mind.

"Get me some dry cow dung!" commanded Will, taking up a piece himself.

Thomas looked and brought some to Will who crushed it up and stuffed it into the bag he had made.

"Now mek me get couple tumble-bugs," said Will to the interested Thomas. After they had expended some time and patience they found and then killed five or six tumble-bugs, a sort of black beetle. The dead bodies of these Will stuffed also into the bag, leaving one, after he had tied up the mouth of the bag, exposed to view. He then announced that it was ready.

"Dat quite sufficient!" said Will looking approvingly at his handiwork, "mek we drive up de mule same time." By searching along the paths that went about the pasture, they at last found the two animals. They watered them at the stone trough which lay at one side below the tank and which they had filled some time before by means of a chain pump. The boys then drove the animals before them along the path which led towards the big house; a "backra" house as it is called. After ten minutes walking, the mules being in advance passed through an opening between the two stone walls that bounded the pasture. This opening formed the entrance to the common that surrounded the house. The boys put up the draw rails that blockaded the opening and then turned to a stile that went over the high wall near by. Will climbed over and jammed a pole that he had cut coming, with his cutlass or machete, into the ground near the lower step. The pole had a small crotch at the top. He tied the bag carefully to the crotch, letting it hang free about a foot. Its height from the ground was about four feet. He stepped back and observed it with satisfaction.

"Well if dat doan favour someting like what Ole Shaw talk bout, I doan know nutten," he said emphatically.

"It sure fetch him," said Thomas, "but how we going know bout it?"

"Tell you what Thomas," said Will, "me an you will come yah dis ebening, when we going for cows and hide ina de bush where we can see him."

"Arlright!" agreed Thomas. After a few touches to the pole and bag, Will left with Thomas to take the mules up to the house.

At this time Ole Shaw and a gang of ten or twelve labourers, chiefly women, lay about the tank on the grass, eating their breakfast. If Thomas had been there he would have verified Will's words, for Shaw was amusing the less credulous assembly with some obeah stories. He was a brown man with an oldish face, large and given to various speculations in thought. He was a good headman, as the foreman in the country is called, but had this weakness. It is a weakness that all black people have; it is, however, hidden and crushed more or less by civilisation and only shows itself in secret.

Ole Shaw gave vent to his opinions publicly and openly and was known to go and consult obeahman.

"You can smile and wink you eye ina broad daylight," said he as he observed smiles on the faces of his auditors at the end of a story; "but who know better dan yourself dat arl o' you in time o' hard time would like de obeahman to tek way de duppy dat trouble you, only you doan got de money sometime. Some of it is foolishness, like dere is some people foolish and some people got sense, but I tell you de real obeah is mos' powerful!" He shook his head forebodingly and the audience were somewhat awed and impressed. At the end of the meal and rest which together lasted about an hour, Shaw urged them up to work and they were soon busy again at their task which was the building of a stone wall, the men building and the women carrying the stones. These walls or fences are very like the walls in certain parts of England. They are built of loose stones, large and small, closely packed together till they reach the height of four or five feet, being two or three feet broad at the base, and growing narrower at the top.

At five o'clock or there about, Ole Shaw declared time to knock off, whereupon the women and men took their departure across the pasture, chattering loudly and cheerfully as their wont. Ole Shaw left to walk up to the house alone. Of this fact Will was well aware. Shaw went along the path the boys had taken, with his loose gait and grave manner, speculating idly on many things. The sun had not set when he drew near the stile, but the day had grown gloomy and heavy clouds darkened the sky. He reached the stile and, as he was stepping up to the first bar, he hit it violently with his toe, cutting the flesh open. Like most of his fellows, he went barefooted. The blow caused him pain, but as he mounted another step and looked over, he saw the bag with the beetle hanging from the pole. Ole Shaw gazed for one terrified and breathless second on it, then jumped high in the air off the stile and back into the pasture, emitting a loud yell at the same time, "Lord, me God, I'm a dead man!" He stopped not, nor paused, but ran sharply up the path in spite of his bleeding toe. He went all the way back to the tank, then took a path at right angles, and went some distance till he came out on the main road. By this broad and open highway he came to the gates of Cave Valley. He reached the house at dusk in an exceeding troubled and perturbed spirit.

Meanwhile Will and Thomas had been very much interested spectators of his behaviour at the stile. From the hidden snugness of their lair in the bush, they had beheld the accident to his foot and the terrified leap and yell he had given. At first they had kept in their laughter but after some minutes they had shrieked out their amusement.

"Lord, you see how him jump!" gasped Will, "eh Thomas? Him mus' ha jump ten feet!"

"Ha! ha! hee," roared Thomas, "an him cut him foot too! Him sure going say is obeah do it."

"You right man, you right!" said Will. "Nutten but the

obeah."

After a while the two came out and stood laughing before the stile. "You going leave it there Will?" asked Thomas.

"Yes man" said Will, "suttenly! You musn't touch it at all. Lord, Thomas you jus' wait! You tink Ole Shaw finish wid it. Not him."

"What him going do about it?" asked Thomas.

"Hi, I doan know exactly," said Will. "I fancy him going go see one obeahman about it."

"Lord, suppose him hear about it!" said Thomas. "Him would kill us fe certain!"

"How him going know if nobody doan tell him?" said Will. "Him not going to suspect us. Look here, Thomas," said he emphatically, turning to face that youth, "if you doan want you very bone shake out of you body, doan tell a single person bout it. If you do, well den, him will more dan kill us."

"Me tell!" said Thomas, "I would rader dead first!"

They proceeded to drive up the cows and arrived shortly before Ole Shaw at the yard. They watched him narrowly, but he made no sign, and said not a word to anyone about the incident. In fact he took his bankra (a basket) and started home quickly without a single word.

"Him looked troubled fe true!" whispered Will to Thomas.

The next day Ole Shaw did not turn up; a little boy

bringing a message from him to say that he could not come to work that day.

"Him gone to consult some obeahman," said Will, "what I tell you Thomas?"

That same night Will would have been deeply excited and interested if he had seen what took place down at the stile. About ten o'clock, just after the young moon had set, Ole Shaw, limping somewhat, came through the darkness to the stile from the tank direction. He was followed closely by a short burly man with a curious halt in his gait, which probably was because one foot was a little longer than the other. His face was heavy and his eyes reddish with a dull red light. Just before the stile, Ole Shaw stopped, and motioned the other to go forward.

"Step forward a little, and if you jus' mount de step you will see de ting, sah!" whispered Ole Shaw to the other.

Father Cunney, as the obeahman was called, stepped forward as Shaw had directed. Mounting the first two steps he peered over at the bag. Not seeing well, he went partly over and looked at the concoction, even feeling it in the darkness. The excited Shaw wondered at his bravery.

"Gimme de ting dem!" said Father Cunney in a harsh whisper, "de lamp fus."

Ole Shaw handed him a lamp or lantern of the kind that drays used and father Cunney lit it. He hung up the lantern on the side beam of the stile and then cut the string of the bag. When he cut the string, he made a few strange noises from his throat. Then dropped back with it into the pasture. He opened it carefully and put it and the beetle into a small black pot that Ole Shaw carried. He did all this slowly and with great precision, while Ole Shaw looked on with awe. Then Father Cunney cut the neck of a young chicken and poured the blood over everything. To Shaw's excited imagination, curious noises and sighs came from the pot. Father Cunney, after pouring on the blood, watch the pot for about ten minutes, sitting on his haunches. He then poured a white powder quickly on, mumbling the while. A loud fizzing was the result and a little smoke arose. Father Cunney got up.

"It is all right now," said he, "de debbil dead. Did you see him soul go off?"

"Yes, sah," said the terrified Shaw, "an' I hear him groan."

"Well you doan need fe frighten anymore," said Father Cunney, "de obeah doan worth a copper agen."

"I am tenkful sah! I am tenkful indeed sah," said Ole Shaw, "I tink I know who put it dere."

"Yes, you tell me," said Father Cunney, "and I tink you is right. But him carn harm you agen."

Father Cunney put up the chicken and his bottles carefully and took the pot with the stuff inside. He first, however, before they two went back, took up the pole and cut it in several pieces. These he advised Ole Shaw to take home and burn, which that worthy did. He then blew out the light and the two disappeared in the night.

The next day Shaw returned to work with his toe tied

up. For some weeks he never would take the road that led over the stile, always going round, and about a month later he told an interested group of men the story, one night in a shop, embellishing it and making it most wonderful indeed by the aid of his imagination: – "And, sah, I pay four pound, four pound to de obeahman to come and tek away de debbil. As he drop him medicine and ting top o' de obeah, a single piece of fizzing and groan come out of it, as de duppy dem feel de power top of dem. A smoke, pure white, rise out at de same time as de duppy go away."

To a question as to what he thought the reason for the obeah being there, he replied that there was a man who had wished to get his position of headman and he doubtless had got some obeahman to set duppy upon him.

There is no need to mention that Will and Thomas kept very quiet about the affair for many a long day, till Will had grown bigger, when he told the story repeatedly, his audience always appreciating it to the full.

E. A. D.

Jamaica.

THE PROFESSOR'S JOHN-CROW (1915)

BY E. A. DODD

He was the most disreputable and ugly-looking bird in the world. One eye was closed permanently, one leg had a fearful kink in it from a bad mend, one wing hung lower than the other, and most of the tail feathers had been burnt. Picture such a John-crow standing on a rail, balancing with a sideway motion, head bent, and there you have the limit of dissoluteness.

Fig. 7 Illustration for *The Professor's John-Crow, Pepperpot*, 1915

It was Christine who gave him the name of Julius Caesar. I asked her why. 'Oh,' she said, 'after Julius Caesar who burnt his boots – I mean tail – behind him!'

Julius Caesar had one morning tumbled over into the Professor's yard and since then had refused to move. The Professor had been seized with a strong wish to tame him and keep him, scarcely as a pet, yet as a sort of companion and curiosity.

I may mention just here, that my name is Dick Smithers, working in the P. W. D., and I live with my mother on Tucker road in St. Andrew, and my back-yard is divided by a low mesh-wire fence from the yard of Mr. Grampson, a retired schoolmaster, the father of Christine, and the Professor of above.

We were all old friends. I had indeed been taught by Mr. Grampson from the age of twelve to seventeen when he was head master of Galway School. Christine and I were ever good chums, and it was an understood thing (chiefly by me) that, as soon as I had reached the annual salary of £250, we should get married. Things had been going on easily and amicably, but lately I had aroused the Professor's fiery temper by an ill-chosen remark about his crow, and Christine told me that her father had said that I seemed to be rather irresponsible and flippant.

One evening, I was watering plants in my back-yard, when I beheld Julius Caesar come limping up, and presently he hopped up on top of a post of the dividing fence with wings outspread. I had always considered crows the dirtiest of birds, and here I saw my opportunity to try and give the dirtiest a cleaning. I swung round the hose which had a good deal of water in it and caught Julius Caesar right in his bony chest. It knocked him over, and as he spluttered away I followed with the water, wetting and sousing him, to the great delight of Solomon, my garden boy. 'Lard! Missah Dick, wash him sah, wash him dutty black skin! Ha! Ha!' He was suddenly interrupted by the Professor himself, who came up from behind some mango-trees, to my dismay.

'Stop that, Smithers! How dare you, sir! What do you mean!' cried the Professor, infuriated at the sight of the limping and wet Julius.

I turned the hose promptly on Solomon's face and open mouth, reducing that worthy to a choking subjection.

'Well, Mr. Grampson, I thought a bath might do him good,' said I.

'Do him good!' thundered he. 'It was a cowardly thing, Sir! – cowardly and cruel!'

I answered not, and, fuming heavily, he strode after the offended Caesar.

I told Christine about it that evening at a tennis-party, and she was amused.

'I am jolly glad you gave the dirty wretch a washing,' said she. 'I wish he were dead. All the servants hate him, for he goes flopping about the rooms. I am sure I shall have trouble with the new cook, Eliza, over him!'

The words were a true prophecy. The next Saturday afternoon, I was disturbed from a ten minutes' snooze by loud cries and imprecations to Heaven. The new cook, Eliza, had discovered Julius Caesar on the kitchen floor, eating her (the cook's) breakfast, which he had pushed off the dresser. There was (I use Christine's words) 'the devil to pay after that.' Abuse and curses and cries rained down on the bird and the Professor and herself from the enraged Eliza. She got so abusive that Christine, paying her a week's wages in advance, told her she must leave at once. Somewhat later I saw her, with her hat on and a tied-up bundle, going through the gate. The Professor had come out too and was helping to get her away. But that fiery and dictatorial eye, before which many boys had quailed, had no fears for Eliza, and as she went she shot a poisoned barb at the Professor.

'An' you so dam' well fabour him! Neida you hab feather pon you head! Bald as any rotten egg that mongoose trow way!'

The Professor's head, I may mention, is smooth and red, and almost entirely free from hair, and his nose is hooked. He must have heard and understood, for as he turned away he rubbed his cranium reflectively and angrily. I felt sorry for him.

The climax came two weeks later on a Sunday. It was a peaceful afternoon, between 2 and 3 P.M., when all mortals were slumbering after their church and lunch. All mortals – that is, save Christine and myself, and, as will be seen, two others. We two were sitting in the low comfortable branches of a Guinep-tree that grew between our yards, an old-time resort, and one that we had not abandoned with the coming of long trousers and frocks. I was leaning back looking at Christine; she seemed simply adorable as she sat swinging her feet in dainty abandonment. Oranges from South Manchester were in our hands. A cool wind blew from the sea, a hen clucked gently, and the world was very fair.

'Lard me Gad! Julius Caesar got de white Leghorn chicken in ah him mouth!'

I dropped like a stone from the tree, so did Christine,

and we ran towards the fearful sounds that came from the Professor's back-yard. There we beheld Julius Caesar hopping and fluttering toward the house, a much-prized Leghorn chicken of my mother's in his beak. The chicken was about three weeks old, and being the last of a brood of three, was the apple of my mother's eye. The crow was being pursued by Solomon and the infuriated mother-hen. We joined in the chase, and all of us tore after Caesar, who was covering the ground at an amazing pace. Up to the verandah, then into the drawing-room, knocking over a screen and a tall stupid thing with vases. Here I nearly caught Caesar, but I collided with Solomon instead, and the crow pursued his course down a passage into the dining-room, then right into the Professor's bedroom. There was no time to think, we followed blindly. The Professor, in shirt sleeves and old flannel trousers, was lying in a deck chair sleeping soundly, his mouth wide open. Without pausing, Julius Caesar hopped right into the Professor's lap, and, carried forward by the impetus, his head, with the chicken, hit the old man's open mouth smartly. Mr. Grampson shut his mouth with a great gasp, opened his eyes, and then: 'Good God!' said he. The blood mounted to his head with an apoplectic rush, and, jumping up, he seized a light walking-cane that lay near by and in his fury he smote Julius Caesar. The second blow, by a lucky chance, caught the latter on his bald head, and the Professor being yet vigorous, Caesar quietly fluttered over on one side.

Thereupon I rush forward and gingerly picked up Julius Caesar by a claw, and took him out, leaving Christine to look after the chicken which was not hurt, and to explain to the Professor. Julius Caesar was not quite dead, but I put a bullet from a ·22-calibre rifle through him, then I made

Solomon dig a deep hole in the Professor's back-yard and bury him.

The incident upset the Professor for fully a week, but it cured him of all love for John-crows. My increment in salary coming soon after, he was pleased to be amicable, and actually told Christine that he regarded it as an omen of good fortune that Julius Caesar should come over bringing a gift from my yard.

In our drawing-room hangs a large photo of the most rakish and dissolute-looking crow in the world. It was a daring thing to hang it there, but when the Professor saw it, he only chuckled grimly and muttered something in an unknown tongue.

7 POEMS

NIGHT (1902)

Softly and silent I come from the East like a shadow of grey:
Dark as I follow the steps of the light of the passing Day,
But the light of the Day grows dead, and my presence is
nearer then,
As I wander over the land to the souls of men.

Gently I breathe through the leaves of many a sleeping tree,
And a whisper comes up as they sleep, their murmered
thanks to me.
I pass to the lover who is waiting alone for the message I
bear,
From his love who is lonely and far, yet now in my presence
is near.

Myriads of flickering fireflies out of my shadows gleam:
They're the jewels I wear in my hair, that I may lovelier seem.
And the stars in the heaven above, come out in their glory
bright,
Like many a light in this world that can only be seen at night.

Silent and soft I come, so soft and silent I go:
Darker than ever am I before the radiant Morning glow.
I die like the sound of music, dreamy and soft and sweet,
At the sound of a mightier music where thousands of voices
meet.

E. SNOD.   Jamaica.

TO THE MINOR AUTHORS OF TO-DAY (1903)

A tribute to Writers like Merriman, Bret Harte, Mary Johnson etc.

In a thousand books and magazines,
I have read what you have wished to say;
And I am thankful that you live,
Minor Authors, Minor Poets of to-day.

Not always writ in Classic English,
Proper period, ponderous style;
But wrought in simple words you give us
Some new story just to pass the while.

And in living pictures do you render,
The wondrous grace of women, sweet and fair,
And the breath of brave men, strong and tender,
We have felt beside us here.

All the gladness and the beauty of the world;
You have made more plain to me;
Roused a sense of greater manhood,
Thoughts more broadly flowing free.

Very brave and cheerful is the earth you live in,
Judged by minds that are sane and true;
And keen the pleasure your words have given,
While half our brightness comes from you.

I salute you, I that love you
For the many hours passed away,
In your company O true-hearted men and women,
Minor Authors, Minor Poets of to-day.

E. SNOD.   Jamaica.

EVENING (1903)

The rain has ceased: From yonder valley
Hemmed in by dark'ning hill I see arise
A misty shape that drifts across
The dark, and in the bright air dies.

Out in the East, a few lights show,
Red and Gold before the shadows fall,
While from the hidden wetness of the wood,
I hear the Bell Birds' ringing 'Evening call.'

E. SNOD.   Jamaica.

SOME GHOSTS (1903)

PROLOGUE.

Not long ago in Kingston a man invented a machine for making ghosts of curious colours and varied in shape. At least up to now he has only been partly successful, and one night he turned out four or five ghosts. A correspondent of the JAMAICA TIMES happened to see them and was so much affected that he wrote some verses, which are rather curious and interesting as showing how much confused he must have been. The verses are as follows:–

"It was a wondrous summer night,
  With just a touch of breeze,
The moon with sentimental light
  Was shining through the trees,
And blushing at the sight of men
  Proposing on their knees.

Not in any leap year was it,
  For you wouldn't then have seen
Young people idly strolling where
  They didn't ought to been,
And woman forcing man to say
  Some things he didn't mean.

Now at this most happy time,
  The Red Ghost came in view,
He chuckled like a broken chime
  And ran in manner new,
While coming down the path behind

Was a spectre dressed in blue.

And following close with rattling bones,
  A skeleton in mail
Was riding on a yellow horse
  That didn't have a tail,
While borne upon the midnight clear
  There came a mournful wail.

Red eyes I saw and purple face
  And may be twenty feet
Of body gliding in the race
  Fourth up and three to beat
It looked like some lunatic cat
  Dressed as a Parroquet.

And last of all with wobbly stride
  A white goat came along,
He seemed to go from side to side
  And was uncommon strong;
No doubt because his goatee beard,
  Was very, very long.

They floated up a tad pole
  And then came down to rest
Upon the bald and shining head
  Of a most important guest,
He didn't stop to change his clothes
  But took a tramway west.

They passed right through a couple
  A young man and a girl,
The former thought he'd take a drink
  And gave a backward whirl,

While on the grass she promptly lay
  Set with hair all out of curl.

They went in at a doorway
  Without knocking at the door,
A spinster thought she saw a ghost
  But wasn't very sure;
I guess it was because her soul
  Had left for evermore.

And so throughout the land at night
  Their ghostly race they ran
I wondered how it all would end
  And how it all began,
Was this what I would turn into,
  When I left off being a man?"

      *   *   *

I hope to give later some further details about this man who has invented a machine for making ghosts.

E. SNOD.   Jamaica.

WINSOME (1903)

The blue grey Heavens are in your eyes dear heart,
The blue grey heavens of night;
Lit with little silvery gleams
Stars of scattered light,
Ever shining with a subtle glow
Hold me with their mystery tight.

[E. SNOD.   Jamaica.]

MOON LIGHT (1903)

The moon light falls on leaf and flower,
So different and so dear,
And changes all with magic power,
To flowers most strange, most fair.

E. SNOD.   Jamaica.

A SERENADE (1904)

Out in the garden and under the sky,
I call to you love, Coo…ey Coo…!
Breathing the sweet breath of flowers that lie,
Around and above; Coo… ey!
But vain is their beauty and void of reply
To the call to my love; Coo…ey.

Will you not hear? Perhaps in your sleep,
Beautiful dreams
Have taken you captive willing in keep
Of silvery beams;
And lost is my voice in that infinite deep
Where witchery gleams.

Coo…ey Coo…! Once again on the night,
With scent in its wings,
My call passes on with the moonlight
And over you sings;
But changed by your dreams to an angel, white
A wrong message brings.

Sleep then my beloved! Little one sleep
Soft sleep and sweet,
And stay in that land where the jasmins creep
And kiss your feet;
And let my song now be music for sleep;
Soft sleep and sweet: Coo…ey
Coo! Soft and sweet!

E. SNOD.

NEW YEAR'S EVE (1904)

Once when your feet had grown weary, O Evening,
Within the cycle of years,
You cast from yourself the burden of labour,
Your burden of sorrow and pain;
And you folded your wings and rested
Upon waters pale and still,
While Love and I watched and waited
We two on the top of the hill.

Ah calm and tender the hush of all things;
The short sweet second you stayed.
Freed from one burden to take up another,
One that yourself had made,
Of hope for the future, and new desire,
So lightly it weighed
You knew not you had risen in beauty.

L'ENVOI.

How short the second you stayed –
And Love and I watched from the hill,
We two – with the world at our will.

E. SNOD.   Jamaica.

NEW YEAR'S EVE (1905)

Once, when your feet had grown weary O evening,
Within the cycle of years
You cast from yourself the burden of Labour,
Your burden of sorrow and fears;
And you folded your wings and rested
On the waters pale and still,
While Love and I watched and waited,
We two from the top of the hill.

Ah, calm and tender the hush of all things,
The short sweet second you stayed;
Freed from the burden to take up another,
One that yourself had made
Of hope for the future, and new desire,
So lightly it weighed
You knew not you had risen in beauty,
How short the second you stayed.

L'ENVOI.

And Love and I watched from the hill,
We two, – with the world at our will.

E. SNOD.

LUX NOCTIS (1905)

She sat where fell the shifting light
Of moon and star; her soft brown hair did gleam
With tender grace; and ah, my heart did dream,
When feeling too the beauty of the night,
She sang and played sweet songs.

Sweet they were and quaint, from life long born
In old time years, when her soul was made
Lovely and pure, to wander down the shade
Of dim centuries, to meet at last the dawn
Of Love's aeon.

This I felt and more,
As dreaming on a golden mist of things,
I went in careless happ'ness by her side,
Over the purple hills and to the shore
Whence white and fair dove's argosies do glide.

And so at night she plays and sings,
And ever her face so pale and tender
Is with me to make me dream of things
I have not; only part of that far splendour
I have and must always have.

E. SNOD.   Jamaica.

ARIADNE'S SONG (1905)

O Lord of my beauty hast thou forgotten
Thy days and my days, our days together?
From the fire of fight in the Springtide changing.
To dreamy hours of long summer weather,
In soft shadows of darkness and shadows
      of light sitting together?

Why hast thou forgotten me? am I not the same?
What is it then that my Lord should'st have fled?
Is the light of mine eyes gone out as a flame?
My beauty departed, my loveliness dead?
And my voice has it lost its sweetness, or been foolish
      in aught that it said?

Ah see! are my arms not as white and as shapely?
Is it not glorious, the sheen of my hair?
The form of my body, is it less perfect,
And the whole of my comeliness any less fair?
Why then hast thou minded to shame me,
      to honour and abase without care?

This morn while I slept the gates of the day
Like pearls on fire did ope to the tide,
And the sound of the fresh wave brought me a dream,
And I thought that we two in great peace did glide,
Ah would that dreaming and happy,
      I of a sudden had died!

Knowing, yet hoping, through the long day,
Have I with weary circles bound
This rocky home, and in weary way
Have filled the empty space with mournful sound,

As a hollow wine-cup moans, when thrown
     by its Lord to the ground.

Ah the darkness of death is over the sea,
Purple the twilight fell, purple of gold,
Even as if fallen the robe of my Lord,
Gold on its hem, and shadowed to blue in the fold;
Yet darker, ah God is this robe,
     darker with death that is old.

                    E. SNOD.   Jamaica.

    According to mythology, Ariadne was deserted and left on an island by her lover Theseus.

COMPANY (1905)

The rain falls on the roof,
  So long it falls!
And cold and grey the evening light
  Upon the walls.
Close bar the house; oh Love,
  Close-barred it is:
Not hard with Love for company
  Not hard it is.

E. SNOD.   Jamaica.

RUSSIA, A PRAYER (1906)

(Lines written last year.)

O God, before whose face the stars do fade,
To thee we pray, – Thou mad'st us with the stars,
Forget not then the thing thou'st made, –
    Shine through our prison bars.

There is no secret from thee hid,
Thou hast thy bark of Russia to thy hand.
And knowest our story; – we do as thou dost bid
    Yet scarcely understand.

For dark and dim have been the years
Where shone no light save that from blood
Which we did shed with bitter tears,
    Tears like to a flood.

A little while we thought the dawn was nigh,
We had our master's word and half believed
When gleamed a sword from out the Eastern sky.
    We nothing pre-conceived.

From old time hatred of the yellow foe
Who recognized not thee or thine, O Lord,
We thought to sweep them with a blow,
    And gladly took our sword.

In rain! In rain! For like to rotten corn,
We sank and lay before the blast;
Our master's pride was crushed their honour gone
    And we, and we – at last!

At last he saw, and by the light
That flamed across the great white world,
And flung aside the blood stained robe of light
    Our banner was unfurled.

We see, O God, but by the lamp of War
Shining terrible, and the night is not yet past
Grant the day be near, the morning star
    To rise and quicken fast.

And grant, O Lord, our struggles be not vain,
For freedom of the body and the soul,
Roll back the night, let not the watch-light wave,
    And point us to the goal.

                    E. A. DODD.   Jamaica.

8 TRAVELOGUE

BY PALM AND SURF (1906)

BY E. A. DODD[135]

Each article in the series *By Palm and Surf* was accompanied by a short introduction by the *Jamaica Times*. The introductions are similar so, rather than repeat them all, an extract from the introduction to article two is printed here:

> *The following account was written by a special representative of the JAMAICA TIMES, MR. E. A. DODD, who recently went on a coastal trip in the R.M.S.P.'s well appointed s.s. Arno.[136] The pictures illustrating the series are prepared from sketches made by our representative… The articles should do something to bring home both to Jamaicans and to visitors from abroad the healthy pleasure to be had in a trip on the Arno along our beautiful coasts and that at a very low cost.*

---

[135] *Jamaica Times*, 27 January 1906, 2 – 4; 3 February 1906, 2, 5; 10 February 1906, 1 – 2, 17; 17 February 1906, 2 – 3, 5; 24 February 1906, 2 – 3.

[136] The Royal Mail Steam Packet Company's "Arno", 607 tons, operated on a coastwise service around the island, *The Handbook of Jamaica for 1906*, Kingston, Jamaica, 1906, 442 – 3. The Arno was overhauled at St. Thomas in the Virgin Islands in early 1905, "This is a very good opportunity for tourists as the vessel calls at not less than fourteen ports … She is fitted with electric lights and fans, etc., and is quite up to date in every respect." *The Gleaner*, 13 February 1905, 11.

Fig. 8 *By Palm and Surf* banner for the *Jamaica Times* by John de Pool

JAMAICA TIMES, 27 JANUARY 1906

'Yes mah! as de ship move suh, me head feel curious fe true, as if it doan belong to me, an me feet feel dat light one minute, and heaby as lead de nex'.'

'Same as when you coming home pon Saturday night nuh?' asked a ribald and flippant bystander, 'you nuh know what wrong wid de road, it so twis' up!'

A laugh greeted this, but the other scorned to reply and continued the description of his voyage to an interested woman who was going aboard the steamer as passenger to Kingston. She and I, with the Purser and a couple others, got into the boat and were rowed to the s.s. Arno, the Royal Mail Co's. coastal steamer, which lay out about a quarter of a mile.

A few minutes later after our departure, two men, very much got up in high collars and white shirts, came hurriedly on to the wharf and gazed with some dismay on our retiring boat. 'That's always the case,' observed the Purser to me, as we noticed the men, 'they are never quite ready. There is always some one late, although they never know when I come ashore. However a lighter will bring them on board.'

Fig. 9 *Alligator Pond*

I was starting on a trip by sea round the Island. I had not exactly begun it yet as I was going up to Kingston that day from the port of Alligator Pond, to stop off a week in town when I should start on the Monday. But as I did this part of the voyage then at night, asleep in my cabin, I may count this in the trip.

It was about 7.30 of Tuesday morning, part sunny and part cloudy. I had come down the day before at noon, from the hills, having heard that the steamer would come in then, but on arriving I learnt that she would not reach port till 6 a.m. next day.[137] This was a bit inconvenient as I did not

[137] By implication, the writer had driven down from Glassonby in the

intend driving up the steep climb to come down again. There was the Police Station – I might sleep there. When I tried there however, I found one of the two constables in charge, half of the Force as it were, down with fever and I turned away to look elsewhere.[138] Happily my luck came to my aid in the shape of Mr. S– a very kind gentleman, the owner of the wharf, who offered to put me up if I did not mind roughing it. He himself had his home on the hills but he had a small house down by the sea. I certainly did not rough it for I never enjoyed dinner more than the one he gave me, nor slept better than that night. Next morning at about six the sharp whistle of the steamer, blown twice, brought me out of bed and, after our coffee, my host and I walked down to the wharf, or rather the Custom House, where I was introduced to the Purser.[139] I got a small sketch from here of a bit of the coast and just missed getting in the custom house a good sketch of the back of a female (lady is more colloquial here) passenger mentioned before. She had on a rather wonderful headdress of some thick stuff wrapped around her head from under which three or four stiff black plaits of hair stuck out. I might have asked her to sit for me but I feared the consequences of asking.

---

southern Manchester hills, most probably in a horse-drawn conveyance.

[138] Entering a police-station was not an alien matter for Eddie as his elder bother, Henry "Harry" Jocelyn Dodd, was a Police Inspector in Kingston.

[139] "Mr. S---" was most probably Mr. S . A. Shaw, the agent for the R. M. S. P. Co. at Alligator Pond, *The Handbook of Jamaica for 1906*, 443.

Fig. 10 *A Prospective Passenger*

We took in five or six deck passengers here, one or two being shopkeepers going up to select their Christmas stock.

After being shown my cabin by the polite steward, I went on deck and took my first look at the land from there. It was as if I were looking at a beautiful house in which I had lived many years without once going outside. I had of course wandered about the many and different rooms, felt their beauty and caught glimpses through open windows and under open roof of coloured wall and pillar, but here I was now properly outside, observing and admiring the architecture, its steps and towers. The simile is a bit broad but it is what I felt.

Fig. 11 *Cutlass Point, east of Alligator Pond*

Alligator Pond has no harbour, but lies on a straight enough bit of coast with a small spit of sand jutting out on the Eastern side to give it a little or no protection. From the deck a few cocoanut trees and a single house or so marked its location. It lies at the foot of a high range of hills that rise very steeply to the right and back of it. On the left is the undulating ground that divides the hills of St. Elizabeth and Manchester. This undulating ground is about a mile wide at the coast and rises gently back into what is known as the Savannas. This place exports a good deal of pimento and coffee from Manchester of which it is the port. We spent a couple of hours here taking in and putting out cargo. Meanwhile at 9 o'clock I went down to a very good breakfast, varied and abundant. I ate very well, that is a good lot, for if I was going to be seasick later on I thought I might as well get in some ballast. Shortly after breakfast we weighed anchor and started on our way up to Kingston. I went up on the bridge at the Captain's kind invitation. It was very pleasant up there, being open practically on all sides, but shaded and under cover. The Captain also very kindly lent me one of his comfortable deck chairs as I had forgotten mine. With a fine breeze blowing against my face, I sat or stood the six or seven hours up to Kingston in full enjoyment, undisturbed by any feeling of sea sickness.

It was a splendid day, sunny and bright, with clouds here and there casting shadows on the water and thereby heightening the beauty of the green seas and blue seas that lay in full light. It was interesting to watch the capes or points of the land come in sight and then to round them and go on to round another point jutting out in the purple distance. It was like learning geography in the most interesting way.

There are those who like only or best the most gorgeous colours Nature can give them, but here nothing could be more exquisite than the sea-greens and purples that lay delicate in colour on the sea and distant hills. We passed Round Hill which lies at the beginning of the Vere plains and then came to Carlisle Bay, which has an open anchorage, being but a bend in the shore line. Here I could see a wharf, from which doubtless many bags of sugar are shipped. I could see the tall chimneys of the estates lying inland. We then rounded Portland Point which juts out from a low lying range of hills that lay covered with trees and rock and bereft, it seemed to me, of human beings or habitation. We had now to keep out more to sea on account of reefs and cays which lay in the direction of Old Harbour. The cays, a few small islands covered in some cases with green bush or mangrove, looked pretty with their fringe of white foam and sand. I forgot to mention that Carlisle Bay is interesting as the place where the Colonial Militia in the end of the Seventeenth Century defeated and drove back to their ship, with great loss, the French who had been harassing the north and east coasts.

We were now going more or less direct east but suddenly we turned towards north-east and headed for Kingston. There was rain and mist among the mountains, for they were nearly hidden from our sight until we had got near Port Royal. The approach into the Harbour has often been described by writers, who are struck with the beauty of the mountains, and their perfect modelling, if I may use a word employed by artists. The sun was just about to set when we passed Port Royal and were going up the harbour. I could see the dark rain falling upon the distant tops of the hills and they looked cold and lonely in the evening. Between two hills in a sort of cleft suddenly appeared a small rainbow which was strange and lovely amongst the dark mountains. We passed Fort Augusta, one of the most unhealthy looking places in Jamaica to me, and I believe it has lived up (or died) to that idea in times past. We began to draw nigh to the wharves and I could see, from the bridge, the deck passengers fixing up themselves and pressing out with their hands their creased dresses and clothes to go ashore. She with the wonderful headdress was now wearing a white hat under which the black hair stood out more stiffly and prominently than ever.

We drew on a level with the wharf and then were brought slowly alongside just as it was growing dusk. The gang way was brought and laid and presently I was driving away in a bus to spend the week with my friends and anticipating already the further continuation of my trip next week.

JAMAICA TIMES, 3 FEBRUARY 1906

On Monday night at half past eight I was again aboard the *Arno*. I leaned over the rail talking to the Third Engineer while I watched the cargo being taken in.

'We are full up to the top,' said he to me. 'It is a good thing that there was this other ship, the *Revel*, to take some of the cargo. She has taken what there was for Port Antonio, so we shall not call there this trip.'[140]

The good humoured chaff and talk of the men, mingled with the rattle of the winches, went on. I amused myself by guessing at the different parcels that were being shipped for the holiday business. There were boxes of oil, soap, flour, cornmeal, all these I knew and recognized by their outward appearance – and boxes of other and larger build that doubtless contained miscellaneous pleasure such as squibs, trumpets, luck-bags, dolls and everything that you might think of for presents.

I went presently to the other side of the ship, and looked out over the harbour which lay in dark shadow with scattered lights of ships and boats about. A German warship lay some little distance away, and her many lights wriggled

---

[140] *The Gleaner*, Tuesday, 19 December 1905, 11: "The Royal Mail steamer Arno was set down to sail from Kingston last night for the outports, western route. The Reval will sail this evening for the outports, on the eastern route."

and flashed like golden snakes in the water. I saw also the *Port Kingston*, which I recognised from her position, for the night was very dark with heavy clouds in the sky.

Our ship was to sail at about ten, but at about half past nine, I went below to my cabin and in spite of noise of winch and chain, I fell asleep before the ship started. I awoke at about five next morning and looking through the port hole I recognised familiar land and was not surprised to hear the whistle blown a little later on, to acquaint Alligator Pond that we had arrived and were impatient to be off.

Fig. 12 *Pedro Bluff*

As of course I knew this place well, I did not go ashore. We took in a load of pimento, and were off at about ten. After leaving the narrow bit of undulating land between the two ranges of hills, the country becomes very rocky and steep. The hills rise sharply and precipitously from the sea and there are huge boulders scattered along the shore line till we round Pedro Bluff, (see page 3 last week's issue). One bit in particular I noticed and took a sketch of. It was a white, precipitous looking rock on the side of the hill, bereft of vegetation, and about two or three hundred feet high. All along here, save for one little fishing village near Alligator Pond, seems bereft of human dwelling. Doubtless it is too rocky and too scanty of soil to produce sufficient for people who are accustomed to a land that gives much for little. We now began to draw near Pedro Bluff which is the most picturesque of all the points of the Island. It is a curved headland rising about two hundred feet from the sea and girt with huge boulders at the base. In itself it is like a huge boulder having very little vegetation. With a line of white foam at its base where the sea dashes against the rocks, it is in fine contrast to the lovely sapphire and emerald of sunlit water. The sea was a source of unending joy and wonder to me. When the sun sent abroad its warm yellow light in the middle of the day, there was a perfect mingling of purple, green and deep blue against the light but warm sky. And always there was a strong fresh breeze, bending the sail of some passing fishing boat, and flecking the blue waves with crest of white foam. Right round the trip, it was very cool and pleasant, if we slept at any port, there was always a cool wind from the mountains and at no time was it rough. As soon as we passed the Bluff the country showed signs of more human life and habitation. I saw the Pedro village and through glasses I could see the houses of Potsdam School that stands on the crest of the high hills that overlook the Pedro plains. We skirted these plains and got into Black River at one o'clock. As in nearly all the ports we lay out some distance from shore, it being very shallow all about.

There was a sailing vessel, three masted, in harbour come for logwood. I thought to myself that a sailing vessel was certainly more picturesque than a steamer. From the ship Black River did not look very prepossessing. I went ashore with the Purser and while we were in the boat a conversation between two passengers interested me. The cause of their talk was a woman who was sea sick in the boat, rather disagreeably so to one of the two who was a yellow faced man with black hair and scanty twisted beard protruding from his chin. He was sitting near the woman.

'Chu, ugh!' said he with disgust, 'wah mek de woman so sick?'

The other man, sitting across, sympathized with him but added, 'I should seh nothing myself doh, for I sick myself last night dat way, dat I miserable, till I want to dead. An eben now me stomach doan feel right.'

The other man looked at him, rather contemptuously I thought, or perhaps in a superior way; 'Well look at dat! I been travelling now pon sea for tree weeks and not one time I feel bad.'

'It suit you well den,' said the other, 'as fe me gimme de train. It safe pon lan' all de time.'

'De train!' exclaimed he with the scraggy head, 'Meck me tell you, dat de train is more danger dan the sea – when you run into anoder engine, where is you? Mash up to pieces.'

'Uhn! Uhn!' grunted the other. 'But all de same gimme de train.'

'Chu! Man,' said the yellow faced man, 'You should neber ah been a man! You should ah born a woman.'

'Should ah been Sir! Should ah been!' which mild answer surprised me exceedingly, but I put it down to his feeling rather unwell as regards his stomach. He will be a very brave man who will fight when his stomach is upset. While we were some distance from shore, a cap blew off into the sea from a passenger in the back of the boat. The Purser said he would have stopped to get it but there was (obviously) too much sea on. The man was rather rueful, but took it philosophically and indeed some one did remark that it would probably come ashore two or three miles further down.

We passed under the bridge that goes over the Black River at its mouth and got ashore a few yards on. There seemed to be a lot of mangrove about, growing close down to the river. I walked over the bridge which was plentifully enough strewn with people who did us the honour of coming to see us arrive, and passed into the town. Black River consists of one street which runs parallel to the shore line and is divided from it by one width of houses. The place seemed busy and bright enough preparing for Christmas, but there was (pardon me, ye who are interested) a shabby look about this town and also Savanna-la-Mar. The nicest houses I believe, are out of the town. This end of the Island seemed much drier than any other part. I walked round the church and along the sea road, the continuation of the street, for a little way, but it was warm and dusty, so I soon turned back and presently was back again in the boat and being rowed to the ship. There is a great deal of logwood shipped here.

There were some Guinea fowls in the bottom of the boat for the Captain and they uttered their plaintive note now and then. To me, they looked like nothing so much as little old ladies in grey. The fancy pleased me, and it was heightened as their gay dress moved aside to show their fair white petticoats. In the afternoon we took in and put out cargo and finishing this late enough, we slept the night here. The *Delta*, the Elder Dempster coasting vessel came in a few hours after us.[141]

Black River, which is prosperous enough to have electric light, looked more interesting at night. You see seven lights – I think it was seven – at equal distances apart, parallel to the water's edge, these marking the length of the town doubtless.

We left next morning before sunrise and were in Savanna-la-Mar about six, the *Delta* being with us.

While sketching I missed the Purser's boat and went ashore in a lighter. Savanna-la-Mar I found different to Black River in that its principal street was perpendicular to the coast right inland. It must have been more prosperous at one time, which fact can be remarked of nearly all the sea ports on the western side of the Island. Walking a little way up this street from the wharf I noticed that the side streets, off shoots of the thoroughfare at right angles, went along for about a hundred yards or so then ended abruptly in thick mangrove bush. I was told however by one who knew that the more inland part of the town to which I did not go, was more prosperous and better looking.

I turned back and went to the wharf as I wished to sketch the remains of an old fort on which stood the Water Police Station. This is the prettiest little bit about the place with its neat cottage and a large seagrape tree and just a little

141 *The Gleaner*, Tuesday, 19 December 1905, 15, "S.S. Delta sails from Kingston to outports on Tuesday 19th December, at 6 a.m. on the western route."

bit of green sward nicely kept. All this being on a jutting bit of old masonry and rock and washed by the sea. The little bit of green sward was what set it off. Is there anything pleasanter in this world or more conducive to pleasant thought than a bit of fresh green grass lying in the sun with a blue shadow across it?

Fig. 13 *Water Police Station and Old Fort, Sav-la-Mar*

As the Purser's boat had already gone back to the ship I hired a canoe to take me aboard. On my way back to the wharf I had enquired of a man who owned a boat and who volunteered to put me back, for what he would do it. He said six shillings as I was a gentleman, which of course I refused as a gentleman. I got another canoe later on for a shilling which truly was some reduction.

JAMAICA TIMES, 10 FEBRUARY 1906

'The sky is blue, and the fresh wind blows

The flying spray about the coral reef;
And yellow with gold, the palm tree shows
The trembling curve of its swaying leaf,
With shafts of opal the whole world glows, –
Jewelled arrows from a teaming sheaf.'

I found on my return to the ship in the canoe, that breakfast was ready. And a good breakfast too; – we took to one another cheerfully. The *Delta* having less cargo than we for this port, went on before us, leaving about nine o'clock. There was also a three-masted barque in the harbour. I call it a barque but, for all that I may know, it may have been a brig or brigantine, or any other sort of sailing vessel, but it pleased me to call it a barque so let it be.

Fig. 14 *Negril Lighthouse*

On leaving Savanna-la-Mar the land rises somewhat along the coast and is not so flat looking, being a series of easily inclined hills. We headed straight down past Negril's lighthouse. There was a bit of a swell along here and it was fine to see the ship's prow rise and fall into the oncoming blue wave. There was a remarkable change as we rounded Negril point however; for the sea now was protected and only ran gaily and lightly towards the shore. Negril light house, of which I got a small sketch as we passed, is not at the end of the point, but at a little distance from it. It is a rather desolate and lonely looking place in the midst of bush and mangrove. The afternoon being bright and fair, I saw with advantage the country from here into Lucea. It looked fertile and cheerful with a great number of cocoanut trees or palms at its right, all along. We went near the coast, which was only two or three hundred yards away. The shore line is a rocky ridge a few feet high under which, and over which sometimes, the sea dashes in white spray.

As it appeared, and the Captain told me the same, all here was once in sugar, but now it is given up to pasture and cultivation. Being good land however, I heard that bananas were being grown and were prospering. The water is pretty deep near the shore and the Captain pointed out a jutting rock to me, which in times past was used as a wharf, for a big enough vessel could go alongside and take off the bags of sugar or puncheons of rum. We got into Lucea at half past three.

There is, I think, the prettiest harbour of the Island. It is shaped like a horse shoe. On the southern end of this shoe, are the old barracks, the Inspector of Police's quarters and other buildings, and on the other end looking across are cocoanut trees and one or two thatched huts. The town, which seemed to be all along the water's edge from the mouth of the harbour, looked amazingly bright and cheerful. Behind was the semi-circle of hills dotted with houses, and very thickly sprinkled with cocoanut palms.

A bit of the white high road showed coming in a curve from the hills and there were some houses with bright red roofs. It is a perfectly sheltered harbour and the olive water rippled smoothly in the afternoon sun. Lucea of course is well known for its yams and I think we shipped some to be sold in Kingston or sent down to Panama. What took my eye was the great number of cocoanut palms all about here, but in fact from Negril round to Morant Bay there is this fringe of waving green and gold.

Figs. 15 and 16 *Two Views of Lucea, Hanover*

We did not stay here long as the lighters were quick and in an hour's time we passed between the jutting ends of the shoe and rounded the northern spit, leaving the white sails and red roofs behind.

Fig. 17 *Montego Bay*

We got to our moorings in Montego Bay just as it was getting dusk. Before we got in on our way up, there was a beautiful sun set over the hills towards Lucea. The sun had gone down, and over the purple hills and sea the after glow came. Bright gold it was rising into red and blue, then the brightness faded into rose and old gold and the hills grew darker and the sea more misty. A perfect quiet of colour and sound rested on land and sea.

The *Delta* came in about a half an hour after us, though we started at the same time.

As it was dark and as I had been in Montego Bay before, I did not go ashore. After dinner I went upon the bridge. It was deliciously cool up there with the night breeze blowing freshly against my face, as I leant over the rail and looked at the lights of the town. The glamour of the place kept me up there for a couple of hours and then I went to bed after a little reading. I read from books on the trip, and I think they were happily chosen. They were – 'Negro Humour' [and] 'Negro Nobodies' by writers of this side of the world dealing with the West Indian negro, and a book of short stories of the life and fable of South Sea Islanders by [Robert Louis] Stevenson, and 'The Prospector,' by Ralph Connor.[142] The reader may enquire doubtfully of the fitness of the last one, but I may remark that its fitness lay in its contrast. It was pleasant to read of cold, intensely cold lands and icy weather while lying in a deck chair wholly conscious of blue seas and bright sun.

We left Montego Bay in the early dawn and arrived at Falmouth at about six o'clock. We had taken in and put out cargo at the former port in the night which enabled us to get away early. I may say that Montego Bay is intensely pretty with the Bogue Islands and sheltered water. The town is more or less girt with low hills and there is a very interesting old church with fine mahogany seats, and a beautiful statue of a lady, Rosa Palmer, whose memory I believe is of ill repute. Some months before I had stayed a night at a lodging house on the top of a hill looking steeply over the bay – this is now the Montego Bay hotel – and I had enjoyed the view from its verandah. This view is very beautiful in the early morning and late evening. There are a good many sugar estates along the coast to Falmouth and truly this side of the Island is the most tropical looking.

---

[142] Almost certainly, the first two books mentioned were: *Negro humour* by J. Graham Cruickshank (Demerara: "The Argosy" Company, 1905), and *Negro Nobodies* by Noel de Montagnac (London: T. Fisher Unwin, 1899).

Fig. 18 *A Falmouth Drogher*

Falmouth in the early morning looked interesting, for we were pretty close in and we could see dwellings and houses plainly in detail. Here blasting had been going on for some time to clear the entrance way of reefs, but there is not much protection, and the harbour is dangerous in rough weather. There was much damage done here in the last hurricane by wind and sea, and by reason of inability and lack of means to repair, many of the houses looked very shabby when I was there some months after.

I kept an interested eye during the trip on the deck passengers who occupied the stern end of the ship. Everybody had his or her deck chair in which he or she sprawled in sleepy abandon till the port was reached. One stout old lady had a canvas stretcher and made herself quite at home. It is quite cheap for them to go to and from the various ports, and doubtless they get besides their trip no little prestige and repute as travellers, which served to some purpose when they are inland. There was one little fox terrier tied out on the deck that had come on as passenger at Kingston. She looked very miserable and unhappy the first two days, but on the third day she plucked up courage and spirit and having got loose of her fetter was running about cheerfully. She left us at Dry Harbour or St. Ann's Bay.

We finished with Falmouth a little after breakfast and started away, after the *Delta* who was about a half an hour's steaming ahead of us. We were keenly desirous of getting into Dry Harbour before her but the issue seemed doubtful as the distance was not great. The desire arose from the fact that there was but one agent for the two companies at that harbour and which ever ship got in first obtained the use of the lighters, of which there were but three small ones; the winch on shore and the boats themselves being worked by some of the oldest and slowest men in the world, as one of the officers remarked to me. At sea, and aboard ship you take interest in anything, and here was a race which concerned us all so we were excited in some degree. The *Delta* had gone out first pretty far out to sea, – why, I did not know, but as we drew nearer, she turned more towards land and by her thus taking a longer way, she doubtless gave us a little advantage. We crept surely on her and just before we were abreast Rio Bueno we drew level with her stern and our captain triumphantly made the *Arno* give one sharp whistle to tell them to clear out of our way, which thing delighted us. We passed her quite closely and we gazed cheerfully across at one another. The *Delta* presently turned and headed for Rio

Bueno for which she had a little cargo. She would have liked to have gone on to Dry Harbour first as she would have finished with that port and then turned back.

Fig. 19 *Dry Harbour*

We, – for I felt almost as keen an interest as any other on the ship, went on elated and reached Dry Harbour shortly. We passed Runaway Bay, where the Spaniards made their last stand. There was nothing prominent enough to get a sketch of, as we were not very close in. Said one female deck passenger to another as they stood by the gangway, ready with their parcels of odds and ends wrapped in a shawl or perhaps in a shining tin trunk, to go on shore – 'Yes me chile! I trabbel fus rate. But dat's because me ah old trabbler.'

'Fus time me eber go on ship,' said her younger companion. 'Me no use to it.'

'Uhn! Uhn!' murmured the other, 'Me know what fe do. When I come board I bring little sweet rum and water ena one shut pan, and when I see any one of dem men dem I know or see before, I call to him and seh 'Hi, coz!' an' him come to me an' I gie 'im a drink out o' de pan. An mark me words, me chile. I neber want a ting de whole voyage.'

The boat was ready, the Purser came forward, and I went ashore with the above student of human nature, reflecting.

JAMAICA TIMES, 17 FEBRUARY 1906

'O'er the hills and sea the after light
Of an old sun's face came golden and red,
And faded slowly into the eyes of night
As fades the light of a rose that is dead.
The purple hills grew dark, the sea was white –
And into a shadowed world, the stars were led.'

About noon of a fair day, a blue sky empty of all but two fleecy clouds that intensify the blueness; a soft breeze blowing from a cool somewhere; a green water rippling gently, whisperingly, enticingly in its smooth white basin of sand; a bright sun, cheerful, and making all things cheerful; what more would you?

The Purser had told me that here at Dry Harbour was a splendid bathing place, so when I saw one of the Engineers going in the boat with a towel, I ran and got mine, and presently we two were on land walking towards our destination which was some little way from the wharf. I found there to my pleased surprise a bathing house, rather primitive to be sure, but serving its purpose well enough. It was made of cocoanut boughs thatched against one another, the trunk of a large guinep tree forming one entire and almost [ ] of the hut. Inside was a rough rocky floor with a bench and a board or two. All very nice and comfortable. We stripped and soon were disporting gaily. It was the finest spot for bathing I have met with in the island. The water was calm, for the harbour is sheltered and the sand beneath was free of rocks, sea-eggs and other disturbing elements. It lay white and fine, and beautifully marked with continuous ridges of an irregular wavy pattern. The cause of this is doubtless the action of the sea, but how it does it, is not known to me.

The harbour is pretty, and semi-circular in shape. A long reef juts out and forms a breakwater on the north eastern side. There is a narrow opening past this into good water and anchorage. After our bath we went and found the post office which was easy, as the place is small. Having posted a card here, we returned to the wharf where I saw an old winch worked by an old, leisurely man. I believe the men on the lighters were also old but of this I am not quite sure.

The *Delta* came in an hour after us and [unloading] took us a couple of hours, or rather took the old men a couple of hours. We left some time after lunch, the attractions of which repast had been heightened, if such is possible at sea where the meal is always looked forward to, by my bath. Some tangerine oranges we got here were very nice and I was informed that these fruit were always good from this port. We got to St. Ann's Bay about half past four of the afternoon. The country we passed was hilly with fairly high hills, and fertile looking. There were some sugar estates, and especially I noticed one fine large property just before we got in to port. Seville or Saville by name.

I had never been to St. Ann's Bay, so I went ashore with the Purser. The town looked prosperous and flourishing and oranges were being busily wrapped and packed in barrels which were being rolled along the wharf and being sent off in boats to a fruit ship which lay out near. This ship was a nice looking steamer painted white, one of the *Di Georgias*.[143]

I went past the wharf and wharf house and walked up Market Street which goes straight from the sea up a steep hill. It had been raining obviously before, for everything, grass and roads and trees, were wet. I passed a large and commodious market which I suppose gave name to the street, and on by a greyish square church on the left. When I got a little higher I stopped and drew out my notebook to make a sketch looking down, as the perspective was interesting. I drew for about half an hour; I remembered the hour perforce, as the tower of the market had a large clock and it was before me all the time. A couple of small children out from school, watched me interestedly and made in loud whispers remarks about me and my actions. All good natured and lively as black children can be, and are. They went away, and then two little boys took their place. I heard them talking about being late for something, so in questioning them when I had finished drawing, I learnt that they were practising with others in the singing of some anthem for Christmas. They were bright little chaps and doubtless did their parts well.

---

[143] A reference to a ship of the Atlantic Fruit Company founded by Joseph Di Giorgio in 1905.

Fig. 20 *Market Street, Saint Ann's Bay*

I walked on up the hill till I was round the curve and into the outskirts of the town when I turned back. I noticed some neat houses on my way to the wharf. Down there I watched the orange barrels being rolled along. The fruit looked rather small and soft, but when I heard the price given for it, I did not wonder.

What I wondered at, was how it could pay to bring a

steamer here to take the fruit to New York with all the expenses of duty and buying? And such fruit too!

St. Ann's Parish is very much like Manchester in its exports and produce, pimento and oranges being the chief of these.

I amused myself for about twenty minutes here by looking on at the orange workers and listening to their varied and racy bits of talk. There was a slatternly girl, an orange wrapper, who was exceedingly quick at retort.

Presently the Purser came and with two deck passengers we took our seats in the boat. One of the passengers was a young woman with a pretty little child. This young woman kissed another young woman a great deal in saying good bye, as if she was at the starting point of a great and long voyage instead of one (as you might say) just round the corner. However, I idly sympathised to myself for I, whenever I go from the hills down to the sea, feel great awe and wonder at the beautiful deep before me with its but dimly realised and half hidden powers.

Another beautiful night! A few minutes before dinner, I saw on a distant end, thrust off the land a row of bending cocoanut palms that stood out darkly silk-netted against the red and gold sky. It was very tropical and characteristic. The Captain and two others went ashore after dinner to a concert given by some school, ladies and girls taking part. I did not go thinking perhaps that it would not be much of an attraction, but those who went told me next morning that it was very good, everything prettily got up and everything nicely arranged and sung.

I thought of walking (by getting up early) next morning from here to Ocho Rios about six or seven miles away. The scenery is very lovely with the Roaring River Falls mid way and but a little off from the high road. I did not accomplish this thought however as I came to the conclusion that it was too wet. The Falls can be seen from the ship on the way past. It was a pleasant surprise to me; – the sweet cool nights on board. I had fancied that it would be very nice in the day but fearfully hot at night. But it was not so. Very nice in the day of course, but the wind lulled not at the approach of darkness; – just shifted its directions somewhat and blew in refreshingly on me through the port hole.

We got in at Ocho Rios at half past six next morning. As my work, I went ashore and took a short walk along the road that leads to Port Maria. As it was pretty early there was not much stir about, – if there ever is a stir. I saw a couple of women washing clothes and I met an old negro who bade me good-morning very civilly which I answered just as civilly. Every thing was wet and there was a sort of soaked look about, like the look of linen that is blued and starched but from some reasons of damp is limp and depressing. The place seemed in my eyes unhealthy and full of malaria but I heard that it was considered the opposite and there was splendid water from a spring just outside the town. It must indeed have been splendid water, if it could be mentioned in the land of running streams.[144]

I turned a short way up one of the streets or roads,

---

[144] The word 'Jamaica' is thought to derive from the Taino word 'Xaymaica' which the Spanish under Columbus understood to mean "land of wood and water".

but soon returned as it was muddy walking. I passed a shoe maker's shop which displayed more enterprise and spirit than the whole place put together, for its owner had it open and was already at work. The shop looked new and bright and was full of everything that you associate with a shoemaker; lasts and leather and awls and I don't know what. It quite cheered me.

This is also a pimento and fruit port.

I noticed here three or four old wharves broken and tumbling to pieces. It was but one of the many signs on the west and north western sides of the great prosperity that must have existed there in years gone by. Yet things go in cycles and perhaps these places will be very prosperous again.

We arrived at Port Maria about eleven o'clock. The sky was overcast and the sea being in shadow was of an inky blue colour. It looked like some glistening metal ridged and rough. A flying fish skimmed the water for about twenty yards which I thought rather far.

Port Maria presents a pretty front as you enter. There is a rocky island with name of Cabarrita on your left, of which I got a quick sketch as we were going out. It is covered with bush and shrubs and there was one cocoanut tree. The water in the harbour is a fine greenish blue, being deep, and this depth near the shore makes it a dangerous anchorage in rough weather, as it is quite exposed.

I went ashore and thought the place looked busy and flourishing. I wanted to see a friend who worked here, so I enquired my way of a man who idly leaned against a post in the street.

'Me doan know,' said he.

I asked a woman, and she being voluble like the others of her sex, turned and repeated my words to another woman half questioningly and then replied:–

'Walk right on sah, an' when you pass de fountin' you wi' see it opposite.'

I thanked her and went on, and as she directed, found the place and my friend. After a half hour's pleasant chat with the latter, I retraced my footsteps and passing the women again was saluted with: 'You find de place, Marsa?'

'Yes, thank you' said I.

'Ann!' said she in a contented tone.

The content lay not wholly in the pride of being right, but also in the sympathetic interest that I should go right, and this sympathy have I found in the black race at all times.

JAMAICA TIMES, 24 FEBRUARY 1906

O, Lady of the South, O Lady Night,
You came in beauty most complete
Of star and sea, and flower white,
And fragrance witching sweet.

To take me captive in a mist,
Of brown and silken hair,
While with red lips me softly kissed ---
I thought you passing fair.

. . . .

And captive ever I do worship
Beside your jasmin'd shrine,
I would not loose me if so I sip,
From your red lips the wine.

The lighters were plenty and quick at Port Maria, and it took us but little over an hour to get free of about seven hundred parcels. We steamed past Cabarita Island and soon were headway in Annotto Bay. From Port Maria begins proper the banana district of the Island. All up the hills on steep ridges I could see patches of the bananas with their pale blue-green leaves variegated with yellow green pastures scanty of trees, for the cultivation of this fruit spreads havoc among timber.

As we drew near Annotto Bay the hills grew higher and higher inland towards the East, and when we entered the harbour, or rather the anchorage off the town, the view was wonderful. We got in about three o'clock. At a little after five the setting sun cast its bright light over the land and the mountains showed up fine and clear. It was a gradation of heights. First a bit of level about the town and river in bananas and cocoanuts, then a rising of undulating hills in cultivation and pasture; this rose higher into rolling hills which lay in front of the mountains not too distant, and back of these latter appeared, part hidden, part showing, the blue tops of the lofty Blue Mountains. The modelling was superb. I got a pretty good sketch of them, taking some time over the drawing. All of this side of the Island is full of rivers. I could see two emptying themselves into the sea, one on the right of the town with an iron bridge over it, and the other on the left. I did not go ashore. I had been once to the Railway Station further east and some how had imbibed a disagreeable impression of the place. It looked then fever stricken and very wet, and I cannot 'bide' (to use a Jamaican word) a wet place.

We were to start from here about ten o'clock at night, not stopping at Port Antonio but going on round to Port Morant. I think everybody on board was anxious to get in to Kingston as soon as possible for tomorrow would be Saturday, and, as somebody remarked, practically Christmas Eve. I was hoping to arrive in time to catch the 4.15 p.m. train for the country but, as it turned out, I was fated to be late and I did not travel by train till the evening of Christmas day.

Shortly before the ship started, about ten o'clock, I went to bed and sleep. I had thought to myself that I should like to see the lighthouse at this end of the Island, and, strange to say, as I opened my eyes for the first time after going to sleep they fell on the lighthouse through the port hole. The light was a revolving one and flashed forth and grew less alternately. The hour was about four o'clock. I got out of my berth later on and, having dressed, went on deck a little before we got into the harbour of Port Morant. The morning was fresh and cool as all mornings in this Island of ours are, with a freshness that is all their own. We rounded the hust of the land and went to our anchorage. The harbour is a good one, deep near the wharf and well protected. When I say wharf, I mean the Bowden wharf belonging to the United Fruit Company on the right; Port Morant being on the left.

I took a dislike to the place from the first, purely sentimental and rising from the annoyance of a detail and not of the place. It is a good place, doubtless, with plenty of fishing and shooting, and rain, for those who care for such things. I like fishing and shooting myself, but just when we were all hoping to get to Kingston in the afternoon we were delayed here for about three or four hours, an unconscionable time. Our wharf was some distance off and the lighters were slow and few, while we had to go afterwards alongside the Bowden wharf to take off a copper retort.

The harbour was pretty with a very tropical air and feeling about it. We lay under the lee of a hill which had some houses on the top and was covered with cocoanut trees all up the steep side. Our load here beside the retort was chiefly cocoanuts. We got off about half past eleven, having heard first by telegram that we should have to tow a sailing vessel that lay off Port Royal into the Harbour. I took this further delay quite cheerfully submitting without protest, as is right, to Fortune who is doubtless of the female sex.

There was nothing very distinctive in the coast between Port Morant and Morant Bay which are not much more than eight or nine miles apart. The hills began to rise towards the Blue Mountains, but just here are not very high. I was wishing that we had stopped at Port Antonio. I knew the place well enough having lived there for a couple of years when much younger. But as it is one of the prettiest (some think it the prettiest) places and harbours in the Island, I regretted missing it and a sketch of the big hotel. Though to be sure, a pause there would have brought us very near to having Christmas dinner on board. As a rule the *Arno* stops at this port every trip but it just happened, from excess of cargo, that she did not this time.

We got to Morant [Bay] a little after twelve. There was plenty of rain on the hills behind and the day was wet and gusty. I went ashore with the Purser but a heavy drizzle of rain falling prevented my usual walk about to see the place. The swell of the sea here was the heaviest I had met with on the trip. There is no harbour and on the steep grey shoreline the water rushed fiercely over with a hurl and a crash.

We went back to the ship in the drizzle which ceased as we were a little way from the land. I could see no particular spot that looked like the town of Morant Bay, there being plenty of trees and cocoanut palms, and the houses were dotted about.

We were off for Kingston about a quarter after one, expecting to be at Port Royal at about half past four. The sea was beautifully blue, with a patch of green and yellow near a distant point. When we got to it, I saw that the patch was caused by the influence of a river. It was curious to mark how sharply the deep blue separated from the brightest green. There was no blending, it was just as if two bits of coloured silk had been put to one another.

The Blue Mountains began to show themselves and the view, as from Annotto Bay, was very fine. It was different from that on the north side in that there was no gradual ascent of ranges: the mountains rose steeply, and the divides and clefts were sharp and clear. One in particular, like a clean cut near the base, I noticed, and just here I took a rough sketch of it and the hills.

I could see now that we were drawing near Kingston for the small scattered Cays off Port Royal appeared in sight, also the light house.

There was one little Cay away out in the light that took my fancy. It could not have been more than thirty or forty yards long, --- it was difficult to judge from the distance --- and a few wide. White and firm its sand looked against the deep blue of the sea, and very pretty too with the line of foam about it. It had one cocoanut tree growing in the middle and this gave it an appearance that attracted my eye. It brought to mind (my mind anyway) the coral isles covered with palms (which [were] always laden with fruit) on which the hero of my youthful romances used to be cast, and on which he lived many days and had many adventures. It was really a very tropical and romantic looking little Island. We did not go very close to it but kept near the shore and passed along the narrow line of Palisadoes towards Port Royal. I could see over into the harbour and could make out one or two ships.

Drawing near the entrance, we saw the sailing vessel which we were to tow in. She was a three-master and, when we got near her and were in line with our stern to her, she began to haul up anchor. This took about an hour for she had an old fashioned windlass. Half of her men would jump up and hang their weight on one brake which would go down with a jerk, then the others would jump and shove down their brake, and so the chain came up link by link.

We passed though the channel finally at a little before dusk. No need to describe the beautiful mountains, purple and gold fading into a purple mist. There they stand fast and silent for us to see, for all time. Kipling's words came home as I stood on deck and watched the darkness steal over them. 'So and no otherwise do hill men desire their Hills;'[145] --- I think we are all hill men in Jamaica.

The [lights] of the various wharves shone out as one came alongside. There were very few deck passengers to go ashore. We had started out with a full load, but dropped them little by little at the various ports. The shop keeper had gone home with his stock and was doubtless at the present moment doing a roaring (I use the word advisedly, as suggestive of noise) business; Miss Jane had returned to St. Elizabeth or Manchester from a visit to her cousin in town; and John 'Smitt' was even now enjoying Christmas with his kin and telling of his adventures in Panama and the money that was there for those who like him had enough spirit to go abroad and work.

---

[145] 'So and no otherwise - so and no otherwise - hillmen desire their Hills!', is the last line of each stanza of Rudyard Kipling's 'The Sea and the Hills'.

I felt a little sorry the trip was over. However, you cannot be other than cheerful two days before Christmas, and I had satisfied a wish that had seemed almost a duty to me in Jamaica. I singled out the most characteristic looking boy (which is my custom) among those on the wharf to take my trunk and, with a merry Christmas to everyone on board, I went on shore. I do not think it is out of place to remark here that apart from the pleasure of seeing the various ports and places of the Island, I derived another pleasure from the pleasant courtesy of the Captain and officers of the ship while everything, food and attendance, were good on board. I went away and deposited my trunk, then, with a friend, I walked down to King St. where everybody was gay with the noise and sport of Christmas. There was one particular form of popular music that emanated from a sort of paper trumpet, --- I shudder in remembering it. But my trip is over and finished and I must close with a wish that everyone may take a trip too, and a *bon voyage* to them.

E. A. DODD

9 GLOSSARY

Bammy

A flat bread made from cassava flour.

Bankra

A square-cornered basket made of palm 'thatch', with a lid and handle.

Breadkind

Any starchy vegetable or fruit that can be used in place of bread.

Buckra

A white man.

Bwoil

Boil. Pronounced bwail or bwile

Canes

Pieces of sugar cane.

Cawfee

Coffee.

Choh no man, Chu

An exclamation expressing scorn, impatience, annoyance, disagreement, expostulation etc.

Cocoh

The Colocasia plant.

Crabbitch

Crabbit. Cruel, rough, grasping, greedy.

Cruckuss Bag

Crocus Bag. A bag made out of coarse material, usually used for carrying agricultural produce.

Donkey rope

Tobacco leaves wound together to form a rope (1/2-1 inch diametre) which is coiled for carrying.

Dun

Something like 'and am done'. Finished.

Duppy

Ghost. Spirit of the dead.

Fever bush

Any plant supposed to furnish good medicine against fever.

Ginnal

Ginal or Jinal. A crafty, tricky person. A con-man.

Guinep

A tree in the soapberry family Sapindaceae, the fruit of which is greatly enjoyed in Jamaica.

Hol'

To get or catch hold of; prevent from getting away.

Kick-um-buck tank

Kick-and-buck tank. A water tank or cistern of rammed clay, in which the clay is 'kicked' and 'bucked', or pounded, inside the cistern until it becomes impermeable to water.

Maugre

Lean, thin, scraggy.

Nager

Nayger. A negro.

Nuh know

Don't know.

Obeah

The practice of malignant magic.

Paccy

A broad calabash with a cover.

Pan sugar

Freshly made sugar taken from the pan at the end of the process of evaporation; carried in pans for sale.

Piobba

Piaba. A mint-like wild herb much favoured in folk medicine.

Planth'n

Plantain.

Premento

Pimento.

Quatty

Quattie. One quarter of six-pence. Penny, half-penny.

Rolling calf

An imaginary monster taking the form (usually) of a calf with fiery eyes, and haunting the roads and countryside at night.

Shut pan

A vessel of tin or other thin metal, cylindrical, with a tight-fitting cover, usually used to carry food.

Sun-hot

Midday.

Tief

Thief.

Vervain

The herb Verbena.

Weh-fe-do

We-fi-du or Wha fe do. A hat locally made from palm thatch; also 'what to do', meaning 'it can't be helped'.

Yaller

Yellow.

Yampi

A small variety of yam.

For more information see the *Dictionary of Jamaican English* by F. G. Cassidy et al.

10 SELECT BIBLIOGRAPHY

Original source material

Cambridge Assessment Group Archive – 1899 exam papers and information.

Institution of Civil Engineers, The: James Robert Mann application, 21 April 1888.

Institution of Civil Engineers, The: John Hugh Dodd application, 26 April 1884.

Institution of Civil Engineers, The: John Hugh Dodd [II] application, 18 May 1905.

National Archives, The, Kew, London: CO 137/499/31.

National Archives, The, Kew, London: CO 137/548/36.

Publications

Banana. Wikipedia: https://simple.wikipedia.org/wiki/Banana.

Barringer, Tim and Modest, Wayne (ed.) *Victorian Jamaica.* Duke University Press, 2018.

Blue Book for the Island of Jamaica 1866. Kingston: 1867.

Blue Book for the Island of Jamaica 1916-1917. Kingston: 1918.

Cassidy, F. G. and Le Page, R. B. *A Dictionary of Jamaican English.* Kingston: University of the West Indies Press, 1967.

Cobham Sander, C. Rhonda. *The Creative Writer and West Indian Society, Jamaica, 1900-1950.* PhD dissertation., University of St. Andrew's, 1981.

Colman Smith, Pamela. *Annancy Stories.* New York: R. H. Russell, New York, 1899.

Concrete Institute, The. *List of Honorary Members, Members, Associate Members, Associates, Students, and Special Subscribers,* September 1914.

Cruickshank, J. Graham. *Negro Humour: Being Sketches in a Market, on the Road, and at my Back Door.* Demerara: "The Argosy" Company, 1905.

Cruickshank, J. Graham. *Black Talk, Being Notes on Negro Dialect in British Guiana, with (inevitably) a Chapter on Barbados.* Demerara: "The Argosy" Company, 1916.

Daily Telegraph, The. Kingston.

de Montagnac, Noel. *Negro Nobodies.* London: T. Fisher Unwin, 1899.

Dictionary of National Biography, 1912 supplement.

Dodd, E. A. (pseudonym E. Snod). *Maroon Medicine.* Kingston: Times Printery, 1905. University of Florida, Digital Library of the Caribbean

Elliott, Michael H. *A History of Munro College and Hampton High School Located in Jamaica, in the parish of St. Elizabeth.* https://www.facebook.com/MunroHamptonInfrastructureFund/posts/714604505338655

Euripides. Wikipedia: https://en.wikipedia.org/wiki/Euripides

Gleaner, The. Kingston.

Graham, Rev. J. W., M.A., and Redcam, Tom. *Round the Blue Light.* Jamaica Times, 1918.

Handbook of Jamaica for 1889-90, The. Kingston: Government Printing Establishment, 1890.

Handbook of Jamaica for 1900, The. Kingston: Government Printing Establishment, 1900.

Handbook of Jamaica for 1923, The. Kingston: Government Printing Establishment, 1923.

Hart, Ansell. *Ansell Hart's Monthly Comments, Volume 6.* Newport, Manchester, Jamaica: 1967-1969. http://archive.is/TfJS

Henderson, John and A. S. Forrest. *The West Indies.* London: Adam and Charles Black, 1905.

Higman, B. W. *Jamaica Surveyed.* Kingston: Institute of Jamaica, 1988.

Hill, Stephen A. *Who's Who in Jamaica 1916.* Kingston: Stephen A. Hill, 1916.

Jamaica Gift Book, In aid of the fund for British Prisoners of War in Germany. Kingston: The Gleaner Company Ltd., 1917.

Jamaica Times. Kingston.

Jeffrey-Smith, May. *Bird-Watching in Jamaica* Kingston: The Pioneer Press, 1956.

Jekyll, Walter. *Jamaican Song and Story.* Dover, 1966. (First published 1907.)

Lalah, Robert. *Roving with Lalah – Slices of Everyday Jamaican Life.* Kingston: Ian Randle, 2012.

Lyall, Bob. *The Tokens, Checks, Metallic Tickets, Passes, and Tallies of the British Caribbean & Bermuda.* The Token and Medal Society, 1988.

McKay, Claude. *Banana Bottom.* Boston: Houghton Mifflin Harcourt, 1974. (First published 1933.)

McKay, Claude. *My Green Hills of Jamaica.* Kingston: Heinemann Educational Books (Caribbean) Ltd., 1979.

Morning Journal, The. Kingston.

Morris, Mervyn. *The All Jamaica Library* in *Jamaica Journal Vol. 6 No. 1*. Kingston: Institute of Jamaica, March 1972.

Morris, Mervyn. *Making West Indian Literature*. Kingston: Ian Randle, 2005.

Naipaul, V. S. *A Writer's People*. Picador, 2008.

Olivier, Sydney, Baron. *Jamaica, The Blessed Island*. London: Faber & Faber, 1936.

Pakenham, Thomas. *The Boer War*. Weidenfeld and Nicholson, 1979.

Parish Profiles: Portland. Jamaica Information Service: http://jis.gov.jm/information/parish-profiles/parish-profiles-portland/

Ramchand, Kenneth. *The West Indian Short Story* in *Journal of Caribbean Literatures, Vol. 1, No. 1*. Spring 1997.

Roach, J. P. C. *Public Examinations in England 1850-1900*. Cambridge University Press, 1971.

Roberts, W. A. *Six Great Jamaicans*. Kingston: The Pioneer Press, 1951.

Reade Rosenberg, Leah. *Nationalism and the Formation of Caribbean Literature*. Palgrave Macmillan US, 2007.

Sherlock, Philip. *The Living Roots* in *Jamaican Song and Story* by Walter Jekyll. New York: Dover, 1966.

Sherman, Joan R. (ed.) *Claude McKay Selected Poems*. New York: Dover, 1999.

Stewart, C. Thornley and Murray, R. M. (ed.) *Pepperpot, depicting mainly the personal and lighter side of Jamaica life*. Kingston: Jamaica Times, 1915.

Wright, Philip. *Monumental Inscriptions of Jamaica.* London: Society of Genealogists, 1966.

Family papers

Dodd, R. P. S. *Windows of Opportunity*, 1986.

Will of Joseph Dodd, Gentleman, of Penrith, Cumberland, dated 11 February, 1891.

ABOUT THE AUTHOR

Rosemary A. Dodd was born and brought up in Jamaica. Her family had lived there and in other parts of the "New World" for generations. She was educated at St Hugh's Prep and High Schools and King's College London.

A qualified, experienced archivist, her work includes the cataloguing of the archives of Louise Bennett Coverley and Walter Adolphe Roberts at the National Library of Jamaica. She has recently gained a certificate in genealogical studies. She lives in Oxford.

Printed in Great Britain
by Amazon

75269321R00161